Contents

TO BE... TO BECOME (2018) 9

Introduction 10

Ares 11
Katie Granger

Binning it.. 15
Linda Morse

Blessed Be the Peacemakers 21
Alison Rayner

Deucalion's Flood... 25
Paula R C Readman

Electric Blue with a White Stripe 29
Jenny Gibson

For Want of Connie.. 32
Gail Aldwin

For the Love or Roland 34
Julia Norman

Never a Coward 38
Dawn Knox

Past My Understanding 42
Marion Turner

Progressing 44
Allison Symes

Shouting in a Sandstorm 47
Linda Flynn

Ten Things I Do Well or Ballad of the Homemaker 50
J S Brown

The Pandemic 52
James Morton

The Virtuous Farmer 56
   Christopher Bowles
To Bee 60
   RBN Bookmark
Transform 62
   Daniel Paton

TRANSFORMING BEING (2019)............................. 65

Introduction 66
Cat and Mouse 67
   Irene Lofthouse
Climbing Rainbows... 70
   Linda Flynn
Disarray 73
   J S Brown
Everything Has Changed... 77
   Jeanne Davies
Havens.. 80
   Helen Price
Heat 84
   Amelia Brown
Old Masters 88
   Beverley Byrne
Over the Wall.. 92
   Paula R C Readman
Russian Doll 96
   Jessica Joy
Steam.. 98
   Sinéad Kennedy Krebs
Take Your Place.. 102
   Gail Aldwin

The Father-Daughter Club.. 104
   Yvonne Walus

The Professional 108
   Allison Symes

This Side Of Blue: 111
   Christopher Bowles

The Undermen 116
   Louise Rimmer

The Word Has It 120
   Hannah Retallick

They Lied to Me 123
   Madeleine McDonald

Time Will Tell 127
   Michael Baez

TRANSFORMING COMMUNITIES (2020) 131

Foreword by Debz Hobbs-Wyatt.............................. 132

Dolly... 134
   Mehreen Ahmed

The Price of Firewood.. 138
   Gail Aldwin

Chroma.. 140
   Christopher Bowles

Pulling Together 145
   Maxine Churchman

Utopian Trend.. 148
   Jeanne Davies

A Small Clay Vase.. 152
   Jo Dearden

Fishing in Troubled Waters....................................... 155
   Linda Flynn

7

Number Twenty-seven 160
    Anne Forrest
Rising from the Ashes 164
    Dawn Knox
Circle Time 168
    Rosaleen Lynch
Cobalt Blues 172
    Paula R C Readman
Book Club for the Elderly 176
    Hannah Retallick
Growing Pains 180
    Theresa Sainsbury
Books and the Barbarians 184
    Allison Symes

INDEX OF AUTHORS 188

To Be... to Become

Winning entries from the 2018 Waterloo Festival Writing Competition

Introduction

The stories in this collection have come about from a call to submission issued jointly by Bridge House Publishing and the Waterloo Festival. Writers were asked to write a short story or a short monologue on the theme "To Be... to Become".

As you will see from this collection there are many interpretations of the theme. We might say that every single one is different. Here are the best sixteen submissions. The other 94 were also very good.

How did we decide on these? We looked for good stories, strong voices and unusual interpretations of the theme. Literary fiction and drama, I'm told, make you think. If you read the last paragraph just after the first you don't get a spoiler. I guess, then, all of these must be quite literary.

We intend to put together similar e-books in 2019 and 2020 and also publish all three in a paperback as well in 2020.

It has been a great privilege to work with the Waterloo Festival and with such intriguing writers on this rewarding anthology.

Gill James, editor and partner, Bridge House Publishing, senior lecturer the University of Salford
May 2018

Ares

Katie Granger

I was an April baby. April Showers, my mother used to call me. At least, that's what Dad says. Born in April means I was conceived in July, summer loving for my parents turned into unexpected red lines on a stick weeks after they went what they thought was their separate ways.

She didn't stick around. My mother, the pilot. Did you know pregnant pilots can fly up to two weeks before their due date, and away again two weeks after? The letter she left me said the month she was grounded was just too much to bear. When I was a kid I used to tell my friends that my mother was a bird, that's why she was never around. She just had to fly away. It was in her nature.

He was like that, but he was a Spaceman.

I used to sit in the fields that were our backyard at night, watching the sky for stars that moved and blinked red across the night. I'd sit there with the long wheat wet against my back and Dad would come out and place a blanket on my shoulders but he wouldn't say anything not a word. Never tried to make me come inside. Not till I was ready. He understood.

I'd watch the moving stars, the planes full of people on some grand adventure. Crying babies and travelsick mothers, tired pilots. I thought maybe, one day, maybe she'd be there.

And she'd look down and see, me. Wrapped in a duvet watching the stars. Waiting for her. And she'd understand. She'd fly down to me. To be with me.

Eventually I realised watching for planes was no good. Their destination was never our backyard. I started looking beyond, up into the limitless ink of the night sky and the stars. My God, the stars. The only things that never change, or leave.

When I got older I realised that wasn't true. Stars are constantly in a state of leaving. Burning up burning out saying goodbye. But for a time, they stayed with me. And that was enough. So, I followed them. As far as I could. Harvard. lecture halls. MIT. Podiums. Kavli.

Laboratories. Kennedy. Boardrooms. Working my way closer to the sky.

And this was it. From a girl looking for stars from a haystack to this, assigned head of *the* most important space exploration mankind had ever conceived. Ares. Mission to Mars. For the first time, we were going to put men on Mars, and *I* would be the one at the head of the table. Unbelievable. Un-be-*lievable*!

And I was talking with Tom, good old Mission Control. He handed me the shortlist of candidates, a knowing and almost pitying look in his eye. Why – Oh. Top of the list. First picked for the football team. Daniel.

Makes sense. Daniel was top of his class, top pilot, top astronaut, top bloke (always brought wine to parties). Dan, who shares my second name and my bed and his macadamia nut ice cream with me. My Dan. Spaceman.

Of course I was going to let him go. It's not so bad he said, it's only two years. (two years and three months.) I could have three children in that time, if I tried really hard. Spend my time wondering why I've started measuring time in increments of nine months. Slots of new life.

Nine months there, nine back. Nine spent carrying out research, setting up and stripping down and taking samples and hoping the whole thing doesn't just blow up in our faces. I'm not paranoid – I'm an astrophysicist. I know everything that can go wrong. *Could* go wrong. It's my job.

A solar flare. Radiation. Suffocation. Crash landing.

Toxins. Bone atrophy. *Muscle* atrophy. Perchlorates. Boiling blood. Starvation. Explosion. Hell, the rocket could blow up before it even leaves the ground. And Ares. She's the biggest. The best. The most dangerous.

As it turns out, I didn't need to worry about any of that. He didn't even make it off the ground. And it wasn't the rocket's fault. Something much more simple. Mundane. A car spinning on black ice. Out of control.

My zygomatic cracked like the lens of a telescope. Like the ice on the pond we threw stones into on our first date. Making holes in the layer that covered the world below. And laughing. I think, I remember him laughing.

I don't remember much else these days. The world was a haze for a long time after that. Even after my sight returned. Even after the feelings returned. Even after I returned to work. They were all wide arms and wide eyes and sympathies that rushed over me like the widow's veil I refused to wear.

Yeah. I didn't go to the funeral. And I know what you're thinking but, why bother? What was left to bury was not him. It was not, smiles and curls and laughter, and love. His parents don't speak to me anymore. They couldn't understand. The cold box filled with grit was not my husband. He had transcended. Moved on. Into starlight and radio signals. His spirit rising with the shuttle. The night it left Earth.

I didn't go to the launch. *They* understood. Instead I sat in my father's backyard, watching the rocket blaze a red trail to the sky above. His trail. Following my mother into the vast cosmos. The sky itself seemed to be on fire with the expectation. The night I finally understood why storms, and not stars, are named after people.

After a while, long after the red path had burned out, my father came out. He didn't say anything not a word. Just placed a blanket on my shoulders and left me to my world.

The dew wet grains of wheat. An ache directed towards the sky. And I stood there a while longer. Just watching the stars.

About the author

Katie Granger is a script writer currently pursuing her MFA at the RCSSD, which she will complete in 2018. She had several short plays staged in London; *Seven Wonders* at the Southwark Playhouse, *Ares* at the Arcola Theatre, and *How Fast This Thing Can Go* at the RCSSD. She is currently working on two full length projects, sci-fi film *Girl In Amber* and radio play *Soothmoother*.

www.katiegranger.co.uk

Binning it

Linda Morse

My first act is to paint my toenails blue.

I bought the nail polish at the motorway service station.
The cheapest, sparkliest, most offensive electric-blue I could find.

I walk in and close the door of my new flat
Sit on the floor
And apply it.
It drips on the carpet.
I swear, crudely.
And I rub it in.

I rub in the fact of electric-blue nail polish and swear
    because I know he would HATE it.

That was me… yesterday.

A whole, noisy day ago.

I'm not exactly sure who I am today or why I'm living here.
I'm one step behind. Still catching up. Still packing.

Here, Life insists on being heard.
People noise, road noise, bin noise
Pantechnicons, police cars and pizza vans.

Life refuses to be ignored.
Live it or lose it.

OK

*   *   *

I knew who I was, last week.
Last week I was safe.
Surrounded by fields and a garden
With a compost heap.
Worms turned my rubbish to sweet-smelling soil.
Here there are no bugs, birds or beetles to deal with any of it.
Just bins.
Bins with brown lids.
Bins with green lids.
Bins with grey lids.
And small mysterious bins that I have yet to understand.

Bin Men.
My Mum called them 'Bin Men'.
Bin Men come on Bin Day.
Bin Day *there* was Monday.
Everything was binned last Monday.
You went off with the litter of your life
And left me to dispose of the debris of mine.
Even the worms would be defeated by that.

Still… That was last week.

The Bin Men and the removal van were both last Monday.

I can't quite remember how it all happened.

Perhaps I was simply dropped into the bin.
I like to think it had an electric-blue lid.
A recycling bin for discarded partners.
The Bin Men arrive and I was tossed in with lots of others,
    mashed up a bit.
Then we were all squashed together to talk about it.

*   *   *

16

Now we've been disgorged, we paint our toenails blue
Get a tattoo
And get on with it.

Here I'm surrounded by boxes.
The same boxes here as yesterday.
The same boxes as last Monday – there.

Last Monday there, was Bin Day.

You said you only needed the weekend to sort out your things.
You were done by Monday.

Rubbish sorted from the essentials.
Shoes: eight pairs – polished and packed,
Shirts – ironed. Jumpers – folded.
Files – filed. And Pants – piled.
New Pants in packs.

Nothing much to throw away.

Just your wife.

Off you drove
In your decent, un-showy car.
Occasionally driven faster than one would expect.
Faster than I expected.

It all happened faster than I expected.

But, if I'm really honest
Really, really honest
It was expected.
I started to expect it
Suspect it

Reject it (several times)
Months ago.
When my friend became very keen to become my 'best' friend.

Robinia – my 'best' friend, started to visit us
Often
Then very often
Then all the time

Even when I wasn't there.
Especially when I wasn't there.

Robinia's nickname was 'Binny'.

It wasn't until a week ago that I accepted, for all those
    months, my husband had been

'Binning it'.

He didn't much like that expression

(laughs) 'Binning it'.

So…

He disappears in a cloud of aftershave and new pants.
I assess the damage.
Weirdly it resembles the aftermath of a wild party.

I commit my pathetic prettyings to a plastic sack.
I thought they made a home
Actually…
They make a mess.

That was sooo last week.
Sooo who I was.

*   *   *

In my suitcase, ten pairs of jeans, mainly blue. Some
    smart, some grubby for gardening.
But *I* don't have a garden.

Bin them.

Two dresses, one for winter, one for summer.
What's the point of more, if you live in the country?
I don't live in the country.

Buy another dress, buy two.

Books – mainly read.
They can go.

Underwear depleted
Arguments defeated
Phone friends <u>deleted</u>.

OK

I'm living here.

Here, where we're all piled up in boxes, overlooking the road.
Our lives separated by a fingers-width of wall.
Listen!
You can hear every snore
Every cough,
Every moment of ecstasy.
And you can hear all the basic stuff too
The washing machine draining, the toilet flush
All our rubbish
Going down the pan.

OK

*   *   *

I'll bin the gardening clothes.
Buy a dress or two
Buy some new pants.
Definitely get some new friends.

I'll visit my neighbours
I have the perfect opener:

"Hello. Sorry to bother you. I'm new to the flats.
Could you tell me
Which day is Bin Day."

END

About the author
Linda is a Dorset playwright who has had short plays and
monologues performed at Southwark Playhouse, Leicester
Square Theatre, The Bunker and Drayton Theatre, and in the
West Country: Salisbury Playhouse, Arts Centre and Fringe
Festival, Exeter and Plymouth Fringe and Bristol Bierkeller. She
has written four full-length plays which have reached short or
long lists of Bristol Old Vic Open Session and/or Salisbury
Playhouse New Writers Award.

Blessed Be the Peacemakers

Alison Rayner

I'm so excited! I can already hear the crowds cheer. I can't wait.

My brother Hans is beside himself. He says our time is coming. He says this will be the start of everything he's been preparing for. He said that last time, too. And the time before that.

Hans finished dinner early then left the table without even asking! He's waiting for mother by the radio, but he's still in his uniform instead of his pyjamas. Father seems angry. He doesn't like seeing Hans get excited, but I do! He's all wide-eyed and cheery and smiling and it's much nicer when he's like that and not being mean and nasty and pulling my hair or screaming at my boy friends if they don't follow his orders. And worse. He even punched little Bertel last week. But I've seen the older boys do the same to him. And sometimes I hear Hans crying when he goes to bed. I don't think soldiers are meant to cry. He asked me not to tell anyone and I promised I wouldn't because he said he'll take my teddy bear and pull his eyes out and I don't want Teddy to suffer so it's our secret even though I don't want to have any secrets, especially not from mother and father.

Hans tells me he's a good soldier and he won't let the Führer or the country or our family down. I don't know. I don't think he likes soldiering very much but he likes it when the little boys follow his orders. Yes, he likes that very much.

Hans is itching for mother to turn on the radio. We're going to hear if we've won. I'm not sure what we're winning, but Hans is already jubilant. I don't understand why mother and father are so quiet. I think mother is secretly excited because she likes the Führer… a lot. When father isn't here, when he's working late, and we hear the Führer talking about what they stole from us and how he's going to get it all back, she's very happy. Me too. It's like Abel at school when he takes our sweets. He's a big bully. The Führer says that we were bullied and they took all our sweets and he's going to get them all back for us. And he will. He fixed the country and made it happy again because everyone was sad and poor and hungry and now we have lots of food and nice homes and good jobs and we have fun together like a big family that all thinks and feels the same and I like that feeling too.

I don't know why father isn't happy about that. He was angry after the squad leader came with the brown shirts for Hans. I was only little then, but I remember. Mother was pleased because Hans needed more shirts but now he only wears the brown shirts anyway. Hans has such a fine time; I don't know why he cries about it. He marches and sings and fights and plays cowboys and I think it must be a lot of fun! When I join the League, I can march too. I'm really looking forward to that. We all sing in school. Exciting songs about our dear Motherland and our countrymen. Comrades that are our brothers and sisters even though we don't know them at all. That makes me feel really special. But when father tells us to stop singing, I just feel sad.

Mother turns the radio on. There's music. Hans stands to attention like he's the conductor. Father fidgets. He doesn't want to be here but he doesn't want to miss out either. I look at father and I worry sometimes. Maybe he knows something no one else does. Hans ignores father now. He doesn't believe in him anymore. But I do.

Oh, stop. Listen.

There's a really long list of countries that are also listening in, just like us. It must be good news!

The crowds are so loud. It's amazing. There are so many people! I get tingles. Then the Führer speaks. Mother's eyes twinkle and she smiles at me like I'm the most precious thing on earth.

It's way past my bedtime and the Führer talks a lot about things I don't understand but mother tells me to be quiet and that I will understand when I'm older. It's a very long speech and I'm very sleepy.

The crowd roars again and I jerk awake. Great news! Our stolen Sudetenland has been given back to us! The Führer is so proud. We grow bigger and stronger every day and no one can make fun of us anymore. We are so blessed. We truly are the best people in the world.

The Führer wants peace and happiness for all but he says that everyone else wants war. Why do people want war? I don't understand. Even Hans wants war. I hear my parents argue at night about how they don't want him to be a soldier and about him crying. I swear, I didn't tell them that.

They whisper about the Eidelmanns, our old neighbours, going to America and us not having enough money to go there too but I don't want to go because all my friends are here and the teacher told me they don't even speak German there.

I know everything will be okay because the Führer will protect us. He's built a really big army and we're very powerful now so we would beat everyone anyway.

Mother says don't be silly, there won't be a war. I trust her because she's happy and positive and wise and I trust the Führer because he's working hard to make sure everyone feels blessed with the good fortune of our Motherland. But father says there will be a war, and soon, because people are just plain stupid. But he's been saying that for years.

About the author
Originally working as a graphic designer and stone carver, Alison returned to writing after her short film *Pastry* (2016, dir. Eduardo Barreto) was shot and televised internationally. Since then, she has written short stories, plays and film or television scripts, several of which have won or been placed in competition. Her first full-length play, *Salad Tangerine*, had a professional reading at The Space Theatre (London) in 2018 and her second short film, *CC Junkie* (2020, dir. Nick Swannell), is now doing the festival circuit. In April 2020, she joined the writing team of a new Amuse Animation *Car City* show for pre-schoolers. Email: alison.rayner@mail.com.

Deucalion's Flood

Paula R C Readman

Once again I wake in a dank, airless space, breathing in my own condensation, wet through and alone. With a struggle I somehow manage to get my cold aching, unresponsive limbs to move, and free myself from a sleeping bag.

With numb fingertips in the darkness, I endeavour to find the zipper on the tent flap. On opening it, I sit frigid for a moment. The only thing dry is my throat as I peer out; glad to see it has finally stopped raining. The night air hangs heavy with the earthy smells of wet soil, rotting vegetation and stagnant water. I crawl from my hiding place among the shrubbery and rubbish, and pad half-naked and barefoot to the water's edge to survey my surroundings.

In the eerie moonlight, with the streetlamps shining too, the pale stone bridge glistens brightly while the gliding waters beneath reflects it back to me.

Tan is my African name. A lion's strength, I have. At night I walk these quiet streets. On one such forage I find myself standing in a large open space, surrounded by buildings. Within the square, I see a sign that tells me I am where I should be. Upon four huge stone blocks metal lions rest beneath a monument to a British sea captain. They symbolize the peace and stability I'd hoped to find after crossing continents and endless, dark waters in search of the Promised Land.

I gaze at the swirling waters, and shudder. Not from the chilling breeze that wraps itself around me or the cold chewing at my bare feet, but at the recollection of the journey that has brought me to this point.

After paying the traffickers, I'd travelled, with many other men, crammed in an open back truck. We've crossed a desert at a breakneck speed with sand stinging our faces. Next we were packed so tightly together, we could hardly breathe, into an unseaworthy boat. For days we bobbed around, adrift without fuel, fresh water, food and shelter as icy waves broke over us. Finally our spirits lifted when we sighted land. We paddled using our hands and what little strength we had left, only to find it wasn't the sanctuary we sought, but the shores we'd left.

Once more in Libya, the people-traffickers rounded us up, at gun point, and housed us like animals behind barbwire fences. We lived in a shithole, with hardly any food or water. Without money to pay for our freedom, they sold us on; young men with strong bodies into enforced labour, and young girls into... I dare not think what suffering they encountered.

So many lives wasted, my friends all gone. Just a prisoner of my broken dream, with no dignity left. Days roll into nothingness, as the sun rose on another hopeless twenty-four hours, I begin to wish I'd escaped into a watery grave; at least I would've known freedom once again.

Rightly or wrongly, my escape from hell brought me to these shores. I hid beneath a lorry, with aching arms, my lion's strength held me up while beady-eyed death snapped at my wrists and ankles as I breathed in fumes.

Yet, as I stand looking at the majesty of the pale manmade structure before me, I wonder why I felt the need to travel so far. The sense of comfort and peace I'd hoped for doesn't exist in this cold synthetic city.

In the distance, there's a steady hum of traffic, while close by the water laps against the concrete bank. As I close my eyes the soft drips of the rainwater off the bridge's arches transports me back to the fast flowing river, of my homeland, the Okavango in Botswana.

As a child, while my father fished from a boat, I swam

in its crystal clear water as sleeping crocodiles rested on the river's banks. Among the delicate star flowers that bloomed amid the lily pads, I would watch jewels-liked blue birds hovering as they fed on the wing. I recall too the beauty and warmth of the place and the smiling welcoming faces of the other villagers under a wide blue sky, and a golden sun.

Now I hide, cold and hungry in the half shadows, fearing monsters I don't understand.

My senses prickle and I snap open my eyes. A sudden movement on the water makes me shrink back as it comes in my direction. Against the moonlight the shape of an oarsman appears. The rippling sound of his passage carries over the surface of the wide, black river. As he gathers speed, the sounds of his labour echoes on the night air. With every backward pull on the oars, a low grunt escapes his lips aiding him as the boat cut through the surface tension.

For a moment I wonder, almost hoping that it's my father coming for me, but as the rower passes by my heart sinks unexpectedly. I suddenly find myself longing for the home I've left behind.

Without warning an all too familiar sound makes me look up. From under the bridge, an owl calls "Tu-whit tu-whoo," as he watches me and the oarsman's flight. For a second, I wonder, out of us three, who's the stranger here?

I've travelled more miles than even I thought possible on foot. From a sun baked land where the inhabitants prayed for rain, to a country where they beg for it to stop. In this land of great men, with their city of bridges, I walk invisible, one among many.

From my tent among the foliage I stare across the river. On the far side, I can just make out the buildings and homes where the mighty heart of the city sleeps peaceful.

27

Like jewels of the just, the streetlamps shine out like stars into the night to remind us who are homeless that we are without walls, a roof and warmth, we are to all, to be… to become exiles from humanity.

About the author
Paula R C Readman is married, has a son and lives in Essex with a cat called, Willow.

Paula's a teller of twisted tales and one day hopes to have a novel published. You can find her at:

Blog: http://paulareadman1.wordpress.com.

Twitter: @Darkfantasy13

Facebook: Paula.readman.1@facebook.com

Electric Blue with a White Stripe

Jenny Gibson

Little sisters are annoying; fact. Mine's called Lucy and she's always pestering me and following me around wanting to play a game, usually something to do with dressing up or dolls. And I'm like, yawn. But it doesn't matter how annoyed I get she never gets the message. Mum says she's my little sister so I have to look out for her. And that means I can't have five minutes to myself and basically having to suck it up. So now that Mum wants to 'ask me a favour' I can't say I'm surprised. She must in some way 'get us from under her feet'. I think she finds the pair of us as annoying as I find Lucy.

"Can you take Lucy into town for me? She needs some new shoes," Mum says.

"I was going to play football with…" I say.

"There's £8.50 on the bedside table," she says completely ignoring me.

"It won't be enough, though." I protest.

"Just go to that cheap place, you know the one." She says.

"It still won't be enough, Mum. Not even in there."

"Well, put a bit to it. You've got some from your paper round haven't you?" she insists.

"But I'm saving it for some new trainers, nice ones, the ones with-" I plead.

"I know but… you won't have to put much to it. Just do it, okay? You know I'm not feeling great. Be a good boy, yeah?"

"You sure you haven't got a bit more cash, somewhere? Just a few quid or something?" I say hopefully. "If you go now you'll be back for lunch. I'll see you later. I really need a lie down… I just need to get my head down, Okay?"

"But—"

"Just do this one thing for me, yeah?" she says like a teacher dismissing me at school.

And how can she say it like it's the only thing she asks me to do: "Make your sister some spaghetti on toast for tea", "Help your sister with her homework", "Just do a bit of a tidy up will you?" And after all of that she says, "Just do this one thing for me." How can that be right? And there are more and more things. It's been getting worse since she lost her job at the supermarket. She's always saying she doesn't feel that good and going to bed. I think it's like when I say I don't feel well so I don't have to go to school.

Anyway I do as I'm told and I'm at the cheap shop with Lucy. I can already tell which ones she wants, she's rushed straight over to the shiny ones with the bow. But they're twenty pounds. So I say, "Aren't there any other ones you'd like instead?"

She shakes her head at me but then she looks at me for a few seconds and now she's looking at some more shoes. She's picked a few pairs that are ten pounds and she's trying a pair on. She brings a pair to me. "You sure you want these ones?" I say and she nods. "And you can get something too."

Does she know about the money? How can she? I get her to try on the shiny ones but she looks unsure. So I tell her, "It's alright I can get something another day." She beams and we get them.

We walk home with Lucy skipping along to the sound of her new shoes. On the way we play the, 'You say, I say' game where we try and top each other by saying the silliest thing. She says, "Cats should wear bowties." I say "Dogs should wear top hats." I get us a bag of sweets at the corner shop with what's left of my money. She eats the little teddies 'cause they're her favourite. And we have a real laugh.

If you tell anyone I said this I'll swear I didn't but little sisters aren't so bad after all. And I guess I can wait for my Electric blue trainers with the white stripe.

About the author
Jenny has enjoyed writing poetry and prose for a few years. More recently she has taken an interest in short story and flash fiction writing. She is proud that her writing has been described by peers as both moving and thought-provoking. Jenny has attended two creative writing courses at City Lit. She has also been included in the 2016 and 2017 City Lit Anthologies.

For Want of Connie

Gail Aldwin

Summer, 2015
I'm drawn to the covered market. A tang of liquorice sees me scooping a measure of all-sorts into a paper bag which I pay for by weight. Further along, there are boxes stuffed with old postcards. Prising a handful free, I shuffle the images until my attention is caught by the sketch of a grass-topped cliff. The striped lighthouse stands like a midget in a dunce's cap as the waves churn. I turn the card, curious to know the location but the printed reverse tells me only where to write an address. This space is left blank while the other is patterned with loops and lines of faint handwriting in pencil.

Easter, 1964
James licked the lead of the stub then pressed the postcard against his knee ready to write. The turn-ups on his trousers whipped around his ankles and he flattened his hair, waiting for the right words to make a sentence. Beginning with a large, swirling 'S', he started. With the task completed, he tucked the postcard into the top pocket of his sports coat. He was proud of the outfit, liked the flashes of blue on the Oxford weave. Thought it would do the job, give the right impression when he met Connie. Loosening the knot and releasing his tie, James held the end and let it fly like a kite.

Summer, 2015
Intrigued by the message, I wear my glasses and try to decipher the words. There's nothing more satisfying than peeking into the correspondence of others, getting a glimpse into different relationships. I hold the postcard to the light and squinting through my spectacles I'm able to

read. *Spent a sunny day with Connie in Eastbourne. Following afternoon tea we reached a decision.* Strange it's unsigned with no more said.

Easter, 1964
Taking off his jacket, James folded it neatly. Free from the constraints of formal attire, he enjoyed the sensation of the wind billowing his shirt. Unbuttoning his cuffs, he rolled them to his elbows, ready for the graft.

Summer, 2015
I search for a fifty pence piece in my purse. Dropping it into the tin, I pay for the postcard. I want to keep it flat, make sure it doesn't bend during the journey home. Slotting it into my paperback, it'll make a useful marker, keep my place for when I next get a chance to read.

Easter, 1964
James startled when he saw her. Connie still wearing the heels that had click-clacked on the pavements. Her silk scarf trailed like the headdress on a bridal gown that she would never wear for him. She looked so vulnerable, buffeted by the wind.

"I'm here," Connie said. "Because I realised you'd only bought a single ticket for the bus."

About the author
Gail Aldwin is a prize-winning writer of short fiction and poetry. Her stories are included in *Flash Fiction Festival One* (Ad Hoc Fiction, 2017), *Gli-ter-ary* (Bridge House Publishing, 2017) *What I Remember* (EVB Press, 2015) *Dorset Voices* (Roving Press, 2012). In 2017, Cast Iron Productions, Brighton staged *Killer Ladybugs* a short play that Gail co-wrote. Gail teaches creative writing in Dorset. You can find Gail @gailaldwin and http://gailaldwin.wordpress.com

For the Love or Roland

Julia Norman

Scene – Harry is sitting at a kitchen table

HARRY

I wasn't happy when I went up to Cedars house. Ronald had cold food sitting on his bedside table. They hadn't even put the telly on and his face was all saggy on one side. I went to see the matron. She was very brusque. But I gave as good as I got. I told her he might have Alzheimer's but he could eat when he came in. Now he didn't seem to have his strength in one arm. She shut up then and came to his room. She asked him all sorts of things like could he hold his hands up and could he squeeze her hands but he couldn't understand. Dr Jones was there within the hour and said Ronald had had a stroke. He said it wouldn't be good for Ronald to go into hospital as nothing could be done and he would probably find it noisy and confusing.

I phoned David later and told him the news I also mentioned the for sale sign that had gone up outside and he was very nice about it. He said if I wanted to buy the bungalow we could come to some arrangement. He explained that his dad's care at Cedars wasn't coming cheap that's why it had to be sold. I offered him ten pounds a week but he said it would have to be nearer four hundred. That's when I decided I was going to have Ronald home if it killed me.

First I phoned Doctor Jones. He was so helpful he came round and spent a long time running through everything. He said if David was in agreement he would arrange for palliative care so that Ronald wasn't in any distress and was as comfortable as possible. I was so happy I didn't really hear what he said next. I was going to get my Ronald home.

PAUSE

He came home in an ambulance early afternoon, I'm sure I saw him smile when they brought him in. They propped him up with pillows in bed. He's so thin. He didn't eat any tea; I suppose it's the excitement of the day. Doctor Jones came round after I'd done the washing up and we moved the telly into the bedroom. Oh we did laugh.

(LAUGHS THEN HE'S SERIOUS AGAIN)

Then he gave me a phone number to call if Ronald gets distressed. He also gave me this horrible thing called an end of life pack. I didn't open it, I put it on top of the wardrobe.

He was happy that Ronald looked so comfortable and it's true, he did, you could see it in his face. His eyes were much more alive than they have been. The nurses came after he'd left, cleaned Ronald up and got him settled down in the bed. I can tell you there has been quite a procession through here today. I expected a phone call from David to find out how his dad was settling in but he must be busy. When he calls I won't tell him about the end of life pack. It might upset him.

PAUSE

Ronald has hardly been awake these last few days. I sat and held his hand but it was so cold. I had a long chat with one of the nurses. It wasn't very encouraging. She wrote in his notes that she thinks he had another stroke but I said to her he can still move his fingers. His left hand twitches and he can fiddle with something if you put it in his palm. I gave him his father's pocket watch to hold. I feel ashamed but we opened the end of life pack. The nurse wanted to go through it with me. There are all sorts of things to make a person's passing easier; so they won't be in any pain. There's morphine for that and an anticonvulsant, I really couldn't understand what that was for, and a load of other stuff.

That evening I talked about the old days and held his hand. Oh we've got some tales to tell!

(LAUGHING)

Sometimes I laughed so hard I cry!

(SIGH)

Then I stop... and it's so quiet.

PAUSE

He passed away this evening after the nurses had gone. It was very peaceful. I knew he would choose that time so I stayed with him. It was beautiful with the evening sun coming through the window. It's so long since we slept in the same bed. I think it was a comfort to us both. I only slept for an hour but when I woke up he'd gone. He loved me and I loved him. I wish... I wish we'd been able to get married. You can these days you know. He wouldn't have liked all the fuss but I wouldn't have minded if we did it in secret. It would be like we were when we first got together. Secret. I opened his special box after he'd passed. I thought I should.

(SNIFFS AND WIPES HIS EYES)

I really don't know what I expected to find but... well it

made me quite teary. There they were; all the cards and letters I've ever given him. All put in date order and some of them were quite dog-eared from reading over and over. One was a poem I'd written about us. That one was on the top with the folds nearly worn through.

(SMILES)

He was such a lovely man. Although he'd gone I read that poem out loud to him.

It's ten o'clock in the evening now and it will be twelve hours until the nurses come. That should be enough time. I've left his pocket watch on the bedside table and a note for David. David will like to have a keepsake.

(SIGH)

Oh Ronald how I loved you. We've been lucky to be together for so long. Here's to us Ronald. See you very soon.

(HE RAISES THE GLASS AND DRINKS THE JUICE)

(LIGHTS DOWN)

About the author
Julia Norman has been writing for a number of years and has had a good deal of success having short plays produced throughout the UK. She has written a number of full length plays that have been commended and shortlisted and has been encouraged by the feedback she has received.

Never a Coward

Dawn Knox

Edna closed her eyes tightly.

She couldn't bear to see the young soldier's face. Long eyelashes rested on cheeks smeared with mud and blood, beneath which, the skin was waxy and cold. She didn't need to look at him – his image was seared on the inside of her eyelids and for some reason, what had most touched her, had been the fuzz on his top lip. He had been, and now would always remain, a boy.

Tears spilled down her cheeks.

"All right, Miss?" asked Captain Henderson.

She nodded, "I'm sorry. I don't usually behave like this. I've seen plenty of dead soldiers… it's just that he's so young…"

"Yes, he can't be more than sixteen if he's a day. But he volunteered. He had the chance to go home, but he wanted to stay. Such a shame," he said, staring at the stretcher, "he was really popular with the men. Such a cheerful and willing lad, but obsessed with proving he wasn't a coward. They all looked after him… but of course in the trenches, no one's safe."

"No," she said softly, "I know."

The captain cleared his throat, "If it's not too much trouble, Miss, I wonder if you could send his belongings home with a letter to his mother. I'd do it myself but I'm due back at the Front shortly."

"Of course." She fought back her tears, "That's the least I can do."

He held out a small, tin box, "The address is inside. He's already written a letter to his mother, in case…"

She took it and nodded as the captain surveyed the soldier and saluted. Turning abruptly, he left the ward.

"May God be with you, Captain, and with all your men," she said.

But if he heard, he gave no sign.

"Bonne nuit, Mademoiselle," the landlady called after her as she climbed the stairs to her room. Her hospital shift had been longer than usual because of the enormous number of casualties from the Front, and despite the sensible shoes, she had several blisters. Her head swam with tiredness and she was tempted to simply eat a slice of bread and to slip into bed. But first, she'd do as she'd promised Captain Henderson. She took the small, tin box from her pocket and placed it on the table with her pen and writing pad. It seemed such a betrayal of trust to open it, but she needed the boy's address, so gently, she prised off the lid.

Lifting the sheet of paper out, she smoothed it flat on the table. The creases were worn with folding and refolding, and it wouldn't have taken much effort to tear the letter into four. In her mind's eye, she could see him sitting on the fire-step in a trench with the utmost concentration on his face as he penned this letter in childish, spidery writing.

She read:

Dearest Mam,

If you are reading this letter, then you will know I haven't made it. I'm so sorry for causing you pain. I never meant to, and I know you said you'd already given Kitchener your husband and eldest son but sometimes, a man's got to do what he thinks best. But I want you to know I didn't let you down. The men say I'm as brave as any of them. There have been times when I've been really scared but you can be proud of me. I didn't let you down. I was never a coward, Mam.

Please give Lizzie and Mary a hug from me and
tell them I thought of them often.
  I love you, Mam,
  Your loving son,
  Frank

Edna wiped the tears away, unable to imagine how the woman would feel, on reading her son's words. She had no idea what it was like to lose a child – let alone a husband and *two* sons, but her heart went out to this mother, who as yet, was unaware of her loss.

There was a small pile of crumpled, discarded sheets of paper on the table before Edna was satisfied with her letter. She reread it and sighed. There was no way of breaking the news gently but she'd done her best. Her eyes were gritty with tiredness but before she went to bed, she needed to wrap the tin and letter in brown paper and address it. Tomorrow, on her way to the hospital, she'd post it.

Edna had been reluctant to look at the other articles in the tin – it seemed such an invasion of the soldier's privacy – but she needed to know if there was anything breakable. She lifted the well-folded letter out and looked into the box. There was a penknife and a small photograph of a family taken in a studio. An unsmiling man stood behind a chair, on which sat a similarly serious woman cradling a baby. Two boys stood next to the man and on a cushion by the woman's feet was a small girl with an enormous bow in her hair. On the back it said *Mam, Dad, Peter, Frank, Elizabeth and Mary.*

And then Edna saw it. The pain in her chest was like a knife wound.

Right at the bottom of the box was a white feather.

Taking it in thumb and forefinger, she rotated it slowly and inspected it, remembering the start of the war. She and her friends had wandered the streets, handing out white feathers to young men to shame them into joining up. How many men, or boys, had she taunted, calling them cowards and pressurising them to enlist, before she'd realised the horrors that awaited them in the trenches of northern France?

Of course, she would never know, but she would become the best nurse she could be, and work tirelessly in the hospital until the war was over, knowing that any help or comfort she could give the wounded, would be no recompense to those she'd helped to send to their deaths.

About the author

Dawn's third and latest book is *Extraordinary*, an anthology published by Bridge House Publishing. She has stories published in other anthologies, including horror and speculative fiction, as well as romances in women's magazines. Dawn has written a play to commemorate World War One, which has been performed in England, Germany and France.

www.dawnknox.com

Past My Understanding

Marion Turner

I suppose you could say I'm an interesting case. Because at present I seem to occupy both states at once: Being and Becoming.

I ought to point out, I *am* dead. "I'm afraid he's gone," the doctor had said to my friends gathered around my sick bed. So that bit at least is definite. As I say, I *am* dead.

However, since that point, I have also become – become a corpse or a cadaver, if you are of a medical cast of mind. Soon I will be a skeleton, mere bones, then ashes… dust. Briefly, I was 'the loved one' in the words of the funeral director and 'the body', a term preferred by the undertaker's assistant, reverence for the dead not being his strong point.

But technically I occupy a strange place now. I frequently have need of inverted commas, as when the vicar was heard to say, "John will always be 'alive' in our hearts." Then there was the memorial speech from the boss: "We feel 'the touch' of his hand," he said, which surprised me somewhat.

And while I see that my 'future' does not embody 'a body', I have not ceased to be. In fact I have become, without effort, without wishing, I have become a ghost, a spirit, floating about, poking around here and there. I am quite active.

However, to become a ghost is not the same as becoming famous which requires effort or talent or something out of the ordinary, such as being the only witness to a murder, for example, or the last one rescued from an earthquake. No, becoming a ghost is more like becoming homeless – with benefits. I can't feel cold or heat; sun and rain are alike to me. I can't get hungry or ill anymore and no-one needs to avert their eyes or feel sorry for me. I wouldn't want that. Though I might quite like a dog. Sensitive animals, dogs are. One nearly gave the game away with its high-pitched whining when I lingered too long near the supermarket. But as far as most people are concerned I'm not here. I don't exist. If referred to by anyone official, I am 'the late John Smith', which jars a bit, punctuality always having been one of my strong points.

What I would like to know, however (and it appears ghosts are as inquisitive as living people) is whether this 'existence' – whoops, there go the inverted commas again – is whether this ghostly state has its own 'life-span'. You can see that we cannot do without metaphor or euphemism. Tiresome I know. I had had enough of listening to all those ways of avoiding the word 'died'. All that 'passing' and 'passing over' never stood for what actually happens, as I have discovered.

If there isn't an end to all this ghost business, I will always be a spirit and never become Nothing. At present I may be an Absence in the lives of others but even that term suggests a missed physicality. Which is not me.

So, although I am dead, I am back to the state of existence once again. This may change, I suppose. One can't be sure, can one?

Meanwhile, with time on my hands, so to speak, I'd like to think I had some purpose, some function. So if any of you reading this can think of a job for a ghost which does not involve haunting or unpleasant visitations, do let me know. I am ready, you might say, to fill a vacancy.

About the author
Marion belongs to a Writing Group and has had both prose and poetry published in various magazines. This is the first time she has written a monologue in prose. She also works with a local composer writing song lyrics.

Progressing

Allison Symes

"Meet Levosa Johnson at the portal. Do something with your life."

The squat fairy re-read the note from her glamorous mother. Mary liked her chosen human name. Despite the magical world loathing what humans did to Earth, tooth fairies learnt their craft there. It was an honourable job.

"Ready?" Ms. Johnston slapped Mary's back as the portal ignited. Mary steadied herself.

"Yes, Ms. Johnston."

"Ditch the baggy clothing. People will think you're pregnant."

Mary blushed. "Loose clothing hides my wings."

"Wear human clothes."

"Can I use magic to create clothes? I've heard about their shops."

Ms. Johnston nodded, recalling the old lady snatching the last shortbread tin from her one Christmas.

Ms Johnson led Mary to her new home, a flat in a Hampshire town. Mary would be a dental receptionist. In six months, Ms Johnson said with relish, Mary would know *everything* about children's teeth. Mary grimaced.

Not now! Sandy's due back from lunch any minute.

By Mary's desk stood a grinning pumpkin. A whispered spell removed it. Mary fiddled with her right ear. *I must relax, that'll help.*

Mary grabbed her flash fiction book from her drawer

but her attention went to the giant cucumber blocking the main door. On the other side stood Sandy.

"The motif's interesting," Ms Johnson told Mary over their Saturday afternoon doughnuts in the park cafe. "After the cucumber?"

"Banana trees appeared in the car park. Satsumas covered my desk. I ate those. The trees vanished. Nobody saw those. They would've commented."

"I'll say! And the cucumber?"

"I said turn it into smoothies but Sandy said that'd take all week. Luckily, the cucumber vanished. We've not told anyone."

"Wise. At least nobody suspected magic."

"Sandy expected someone to spring out of it."

"I've seen television shows where that happens. Humans are odd like that. You *are* just using magic at home?"

Mary nodded and reached for her right ear only to have her hand clamped.

"You *do* know fairies can summon things like that?" Ms Johnson released the girl's hand as the cafe owner returned. His glare at Ms Johnson would've meant retribution had Mary been elsewhere.

"Any reports on this fine Monday morning, Mary?"

"There's been nothing at the dentists."

"Stop sounding defensive. Giant gooseberries topped the church spire, a huge raspberry crushed old Mr Benson's greenhouse. I sorted that. You're lucky the guy didn't have a heart attack. Stop the ear fiddling *now*. You *are* summoning things, but why the hell it's fruit and veg is beyond me."

"I'll try, Ms. Johnson."

"You *will* stop it or the Queen sacks me. You'll return to your mother."

Mary gulped. The Fairy Queen *didn't* worry her.

"Mary, you'll be an excellent tooth fairy." Ms Johnson said after the pair devoured Mary's Sunday roast. "The only place for fruit and veg this week was on our plates. Anything at work?"

"No, thankfully."

"You stopped the ear fiddling?"

"I tried."

"What happened?"

"I changed my thoughts so anything I summon blends in with my surroundings."

Ms Johnson hugged Mary. "Inventing that shows you're now a resourceful fairy. Well done!"

About the author

Allison Symes writes fairy tales with bite as flash fiction, novels and short stories. Her flash fiction collection, *From Light to Dark and Back Again,* was published by Chapeltown Books in 2017. She is a member of the Association of Christian Writers and Society of Authors. She adores P.G. Wodehouse, Jane Austen and Terry Pratchett. Allison's main website is www.fairytaleswithbite.weebly.com and she blogs for Chandler's Ford Today at http://chandlersfordtoday.co.uk/author/allison-symes/.

Shouting in a Sandstorm

Linda Flynn

My mother sits in the same chair, watching the scene unfold before her. It begins as a murky grey day in which the sky and sea seem to merge. Gradually the tide retreats, laying the beach bare for the dramas to be enacted upon it. The sun spot lights the ridged sand amid cries of laughter, barking dogs and shrieks of seagulls. Colours and shapes flap in and out of her vision, as she sits hunched in a fluffy pink cardigan, enclosed in her own fuzzy world.

It began with a bag. Like so many insignificant things, it gained importance with memory; mine that is, not hers. She never forgot her handbag when she went to the shops, yet that day she left it lying limply in the porch.

I scooped it up and ran after her, knowing that something was wrong, but not understanding how events would develop. My breath caught in the freshening wind. I found her staring in the newsagent's window with a frown on her face. Her eyes widened as I passed her bag over. She recovered quickly with a smile and we brushed the moment over. It was a snapshot of the life that was to come; one we wanted to delete.

Our hair flapped around our faces as we walked back along the beach, welcoming the distraction of the stinging wind. Whirlwinds of sand were whipped up and thrashed against our legs. Still we trudged on with our heads bowed, unable to see where we were walking. Billowing clouds reared up like saffron waves. We tried to call out to each other, but our words were whisked up into the air and somersaulted away, filling our mouths with gritty sand.

After a few minutes the storm eased enough for us to

raise our heads and look around, before heading towards the damper sand. There our feet sank into a soggy mush, oozing into puddles, before our prints were obliterated.

I check that my mother is not too warm by the window, but her hand flaps me away. A bad day. Her cool control has been loosened like a band that has lost its elasticity. Speech which had once flowed freely drizzled through her mind.

At first the words clustered together in sticky clumps. Helplessly I watched her wrestle for them: squinting her eyes, as they jumbled through her once brilliant brain, erupting in a tangle or twisting, turning, tumbling out of view.

Friends fled in tears, unable to confront her infirmity and their own frailty. Her chest squeezed with their anguish.

At times she would have a piercing flash of recognition that lost words were more easily hidden in silence.

I place a photo album on her lap, her past captured as she stood up straight in a suit, clutching a briefcase. Her eyes looked straight at the camera, full of confidence for the future. Now her sharp edges have been sanded down. When I look at my mother, I search to see her in this sweet, gentle stranger.

I turn the pages of her recorded life. Clouds clear across her face as she gives a glimmer of recognition. She points. Just for a moment, laughter lifts her like a lark, singing, soaring higher into the sky. Then the bars crash down and the bird is caged once more.

Her eyes squeeze shut, her hand pummels the air. She is screaming inside.

My mother tries to speak but the words keep sliding off her tongue, slipping away like ice cubes.

Her gaze becomes wistful, far away. I wrap a shawl

around her shoulders although she does not stir. Outside the window the clouds bunch together, the sun retreats. The tide pours in, clearing the beach, wiping away all trace of what has been.

About the author:
Linda Flynn has had two children's books and one book for teenagers published. In addition she has had eleven short stories (for adults, children and young adults) as well as a number of newspaper and magazine articles printed. Her first writing commission was for six educational books with the Heinemann Fiction Project.

Ten Things I Do Well or Ballad of the Homemaker

J S Brown

I can do the washing up.
Rays of light pierce the transparency
of the glasses whilst the last colours
burst on the rims
Cosmic Traveller

I can do the ironing.
My hand on the steamer
sailing through sirens of mists
flattening to crispness a white sea of linen
Oceanic Navigator

I can do the cooking.
In the still of time, I bring to the pan
raw emotions, slowly transmuted
with the flame of my intention
Experimental Alchemist

I can do the sewing.
The sharp metal pierces a ridge of cloth, fingers, hearts,
weaving a trail of blood and stories
into the wasteland of an old king
Errant Knight

I can do the dusting.
Webbed magic wands
disturb settled sediment and ancient particles;
casting spells in underground caves
Enchanted Sorcerer

I can do the sweeping.
Gliding feet, flowing laces, dancing Darcys
on faded flooring,
glitzy mirrors, candles, lights…
Fairy-tale Orchestrator

I can also do the weeping
nested against
the silent curtains of the stars.
Morpheus ceases the counting
– woman, stranger.

About the author
Born in Lisbon, J S Brown lives in London with her family and
enjoys being part of a thriving community in Waterloo; she is a
regular at St John's Waterloo. She has recently been developing
a painting practice by attending fine art courses at the local
Morley College.

The Pandemic

James Morton

It happened erratically, and initially, in isolated circumstances. At graduations and other similar events across the globe, reports emerged of groups of students abruptly transforming into rodents. At the start, the stories were confined to smaller communities, though this changed dramatically in the summer of 2009. Wide-eyed and wistful in attendance at ceremonies, the students would sit through a sequence of commencement speeches before standing and approaching the podium, arms outstretched to receive their diploma, only to discover, instants after their fingers had clasped the parchment, that a transformation had kicked in. Their eyebrows would rise, their nostrils wrinkle, and with a brief spasm, they would vanish, their graduation gowns hovering for a moment before collapsing to the ground, tailed by a series of gasps from the horrified onlookers and keynote speakers. Then, from the folds of the fabric, a rat would slip out, a perfectly ordinary rat with pink eyes, squinting at its audience, and seconds later, the gasps became screams. That summer, the sale of smelling salts surged.

Understandably, the press was unnerved, and the word "baffling" was used in abundance. Out of fear, many undergraduates dropped out of their studies midway, though this tactic too proved flawed, as those that did so were transformed into bigger rats, with sharper teeth and thicker tails. Politicians regularly made speeches about confusion, and dark days.

Before long, the question quickly changed from "How can we stop this?" to "What can be done with these rats?" – or Species-Challenged People (SCPs) as they grew to be called. Fortunately, the students-turned-rats' voices were still distinguishable in their mother tongues, despite being echoed by a subtle squeaking every time one tried to speak. The only possible solution was deemed that they accommodate themselves in the homes of their parents or legal guardians until such time as a cure was found. Younger siblings found a degree of fun in this new setup, though they were constantly reminded that this new pet was their elder brother or sister and they were forbidden to roughhouse. Parents on the verge of retirement were not so overjoyed. Keeping the rats proved costly, as many companies tried to cash in on the phenomenon, selling flavoured pellets at an excessive price, and even modelling elaborate cages with bells and trapezes. (Latches were optional.) Many parents of postgraduates made arrangements with employers to extend their contracts, consigning themselves to another decade or so in work. Cat owners were told to pack in their felines or face the consequences. Ultimately, cat sanctuaries worldwide were overwhelmed with new intake.

Soon enough, depression became rife amongst the SCPs. A unique brand of antidepressant was manufactured, dosed out in pellet form to accommodate the rats' digestive tracts. Its impact was minimal, and reports still crept out of SCPs hanging themselves from their trapezes or strangling themselves with their own tails. But where were they to turn?

"Just wait," came the response. "Keep waiting. Wait it out, for it all to blow over. Who knows? Things could be right as rain in five years. Maybe seven. Ten tops. Just wait."

But waiting proved pricey, and before long, the rats began a generally fruitless search for employment. Though discrimination against SCPs was sternly forbidden, few employers found the prospect of employing a rat appealing.

They couldn't reach filing cabinets given their restrictive stature, their claws couldn't handle computer keyboards, they couldn't use shredders in case they tumbled right in. In addition, their voices were becoming more indecipherable by the day, so jobs involving telephones were also out of the question. Even those for whom such factors weren't an issue were often sent packing, as a pair of yellow eyes and twitching whiskers behind a keyboard was enough to unnerve any fellow employee or distinguished, high-calibre client. It transpired the rats were best suited to working in kitchens or bars, their long tails superbly adept at wiping cloths across dishes, brewing multiple coffees and shunting brooms across dirty linoleum. Restaurant owners became keen to employ SCPs and some even implemented schemes aimed at them in specific, though the hours were long and the pay meagre, and many declined on matters of principle.

Over time, SCP support groups were established – starting out online, then the groups convened in person, in libraries, coffee shops, pub function rooms. Eventually, news broke that brought both hope and horror to the ears of the SCPs: that an unreliable source had word that an antidote to their turbulent plight had been concocted somewhere in Germany. It hadn't yet been 100% successful – already, it had turned a number of people inside-out and transformed others into a mutated half-being, equal parts rat and human, with residual whiskers and a tail protruding from the left knee. Nonetheless, the news brought an end to weeks of despair and would have been greeted with elation had it not been for additional reports that the government had deemed the antidote too expensive to warrant widespread manufacture. Outrage naturally ensued.

"It's a conspiracy!" they chorused. "A scandal! We'll take to the streets and alert the world!"

They did exactly that, painting banners and suspending them from factory rooftops, hoisting placards as high as they could muster and bleating slogans into loudspeakers as they marched the streets of every capital city worldwide. Heads turned, certainly, but by that time, sadly, the rats' voices had all but vanished, and try as they might, all anyone heard as they scampered by was a series of discordant squeaks.

About the author:
James Morton is a writer, director and producer of film and theatre based in London. He has a degree in English Literature from Durham University and has worked as a digital writer for BBC Worldwide, Endemol and Fremantle, a travel writer for Taiken.co, and a film critic for CinemaChords.com. He has written nine plays and made over thirty short films to date. He currently works for the BBC.

www.jamesmorton.co

The Virtuous Farmer

Christopher Bowles

There once was a good Catholic farmer, who married a good Catholic woman; and for a time, they were happy and perfect. They were husband and wife, and in the eyes of God they did everything they should. They were pious and devout; they respected each other, and they respected their Lord.

One day, the farmer's wife told her husband she was pregnant. The sisters at the convent told her by the way she was carrying, that she should expect a girl. And for many days they wondered what they should name their unborn daughter.

They decided to call her Hope. They wanted their child to embody all things uplifting and optimistic. They wanted her to light up rooms and raise hearts, and so Hope she was named.

However, one day, the farmer's wife grew sick and the sisters took her into a room. When they emerged, they told the farmer that his wife had miscarried, and that Hope would never see the world. The farmer held his wife and cried, and they began to rebuild their lives.

When the farmer's wife fell pregnant a second time, they were overjoyed, and again, pondered what the name of their second child would be. The sisters once again told the parents-to-be that they would be expecting another girl, and so they named her Faith. They decided they wanted a daughter who would be pious and virtuous, and dedicate herself to the Lord. They thanked God for giving them a second chance, and in gratitude, they offered her to Him.

The farmer's wife miscarried a second time. Faith never got to see the world. The farmer and his wife mourned for months.

In the following years, they tried again for children, many times; and each time, the sisters told them they would be expecting a girl. But each time, the baby never survived. After Hope, and Faith, they lost Charity, Serenity, Grace, Mercy and Patience. Seven daughters that never saw their first breath. Seven sisters, to keep each other company beyond the veil.

The farmer was distraught. His faith was shaken, and he turned to drink. He howled with rage at the evening moon. His wife was a shell of her former self, growing frail and haunted and gaunt. She refused to eat, and she refused to talk, and she refused to touch her husband in their marriage-bed.

The sisters rallied around, and tried to heal the broken family. They left with their heads low, rosaries upon their lips, and beads slipping through clutched fingers.

One day, the farmer came back from drinking, and crying, and screaming with rage at the night sky, and expected his wife to have retired to their bed on his return. But she was awake, and sat in the kitchen. She greeted him when he arrived. Her high spirits disconcerted him, and he asked her why she was so cheery. She told him that a man had come to visit.

A man, who smelled of money, not from the village. A stranger. He had told her that they would be able to have a baby. He grinned and told them that he was an augur of sorts; that he could examine the farmer's wife and guarantee a healthy baby in nine months' time. His words were so persuasive, that they both readily agreed, and the farmer had a drink whilst the man took his wife into their marriage bed, and began his examination.

The next morning, the wife told her husband she could feel she was with child. The farmer rejoiced, and set about preparing her a fine breakfast. And as she ate, she thought about their lost virtues.

One month into her pregnancy, she was no longer satisfied with the cheese and bread the farmer could supply her. She demanded a sacrifice, and so the farmer slaughtered his prize hen. She ate the meat raw, and smiled. And on that day, she forgot about Hope.

Two months into the pregnancy, she demanded a second sacrifice. And so the farmer slaughtered his favourite goose. She ate the meat raw, and forgot about Grace. Three months, and her hunger would only be abated by the doe-rabbit from the outside hutch. The meat was left raw and eaten with pleasure. The farmer's wife forgot about Charity.

Four months saw her request the farmer's faithful nanny goat, sliced up from haunch to haunch on a platter. As the last bite was slipped into her mouth, she forgot about Serenity. At five months she demanded the farmer's fat ewe, raw and steaming with offal on her plate. She ate, and forgot about Grace, and the haunted look on her face began to lift.

Six months saw the farmer's sow eaten – bloodied and filleted in exchange for all memories of Mercy; and seven months saw the slaughter of his hinny-mule, and all recollection of Patience slip from his wife's eyes.

In her eighth month, she grew feral-eyed and plump. She glowed with maternal vigour, and hunger. She howled with rage until the farmer dragged his best mare to the chopping-block, and took off her head with the wood-axe. The horse was served promptly at eight, and the wife grinned with pleasure.

The ninth month saw the farmer prepare his finest cow for his wife. Eaten raw, as with the other animals, and the last of the humanity disappeared from her face. She birthed a baby girl as she devoured the last chunk of beef; parting her legs under the kitchen table.

The wife breathed her last, sat at her plate, cutlery still in hand, and in her dying breath named the child. The farmer remembered all the virtuous daughters that had failed to live; all the virtuous glories that would never see daylight. Then he looked down at his bloody daughter, smeared in afterbirth, her new name burning brightly with untold potential.

He imagined all the fresh horrors she might bring to world.

And he smiled.

About the author
Christopher has been published in the previous Bridge House anthologies *Snowflakes* and *Baubles*, and has now established himself as a performance poet and playwright. Since having opened his company *Magpie Man Theatre* in 2015, he has seen award-winning success with debut spoken word production *MOUTH*, and received critical acclaim for its physical theatre successor *AUTOPSY*.

This year he is set to introduce his one-man show *Live In Technicolor*, and continues his work as resident spoken word artist with WWI remembrance choir *HONOUR*.

His collection *Spectrum* was published by Chapeltown in July 2017.

To Bee

RBN Bookmark

You may not know me, still, I'm sure you have seen me around.

I'm a bit of a celebrity, you might have caught a glimpse of me in front of the TV cameras… I do love making surprise appearances whenever there`s an outside broadcast.

A freak of nature is what folk call me.

My aerodynamics will make you dizzier than Spaghetti Junction, leave boffins perplexed and scratching their heads.

Awkward high flyer that I am, a full pollen basket and a need for a pee can make it an uphill battle to get ones thorax off the ground.

Excuse me for asking by the way, but hasn`t my flight path bumped into you before???

Born of royal descent, I'm no common fly by night, but mum (God save the Queen!)

Well, she did spread it about a bit, so sibling rivalry might sometimes appear a little fierce.

Yet not for the throne mind, for I assure you that the only heirs apparent are the ones you see on our backs.

At this time of the year things are buzzing.

Our "Busy Bee" schedule leaves little downtime, before it is bedtime for the family and me.

We`re the Apinis Family by the way.

Although I shall never for the life of me understand how we ever came by the Italian name, for we ain't global travellers by any means… We like to keep it local; I suppose one could say we are the white van drivers of the insect world.

Yet despite the Mafia sounding name, we`re no behind-the-scenes gangsters, nor are we hired hit men looking for the next sting.

We are the good guys who just bumble about our business when the summer is in bloom. Then come winter, we`ll drop off like flies, leaving next year`s harvest in the capable pollen presses of the new recruits, who sadly it seems are so much harder to come by these days.

To quote the words of a famous Pollentician:

"Never in the fields of dormice &
meningoencephalitis bearing tics
Was so much pollen gathered
By Bees so few
For the germination of so many."

It's a speech that still, to this day, makes my setae stand on end…. I guess it just sort of sums up the little man.

Well, I have really enjoyed our chat, but alas, it is time for me To Bee going.

Still, one never knows, maybe we′ll bump into each other again before… the summer is over.

Bee seeing you

About the author
RBN Bookmark grew up in the city of Manchester in North West England during the 1960s. The eldest of 3 siblings to Irish parents, he began writing late in life.

These days he lives in Sweden, and, with the promise of an early retirement in the wings, he now hopes to be able to devote more to time to those many unfinished writing projects that are clogging up his pipeline.

www.rbnbookmark.com

Transform

Daniel Paton

The transformation, they had told her, would be painful. Not only painful, but irreversible. That much seemed obvious to her anyway, but they had repeated those phrases several times.

"It will be painful. Very painful. And irreversible. Completely. You understand that, right?" the doctor had said, sitting across from her in his serious white coat.

It was as if they wanted to scare her off. They had so desperately advertised for volunteers, yet now that they had one, it was almost like they didn't want to go through with it.

She had signed so many forms she had lost count. It got to the point where she didn't even bother reading them, just skipped through to find the dotted line.

Then there was all the checks. Every part of her measured and tested. Not just her body, but her mind too. It was all to make sure that she could handle the transformation, physically and mentally. Of course, the doctors themselves didn't exactly know what it would take; all their workings were based on theory, not practice. This had never been done before.

This fact would have daunted many, but not Helen. Helen wanted this. She wanted massive change. Her life, her body – she was sick of it all. Not outwardly sick, or aggressively sick; more that she had become so passive in her own existence that she couldn't see any point in carrying on with it. She was thinking of ending it herself before she saw the poster at the hospital, "Volunteers wanted – revolutionary scientific experiment." How could you not be curious about that?

Then when she did find out more, it seemed so ridiculous that she simply couldn't turn it down. Apparently, no-one else had followed up the initial inquiry meeting with the doctors; they were all too shocked. But there was strict prohibition of any spread information regarding the experiment; the public weren't to know anything until or unless it was successful.

Now she sat, waiting, in the research facility. She tapped her thin finger on the arm of the plastic chair and looked around. It wasn't like a hospital waiting room, that's spacious but crowded, with beige walls and old magazines, this was just a few chairs around a table near the small reception desk. She figured it wasn't supposed to be a waiting room, but just that they weren't ready for her yet and needed to keep her out of the way until they were. Somewhere on the floor above, they were manically rushing around to get everything set up and ready. She had one more document to sign, and then the procedures would begin.

This gave her a while to reflect on her 43 years as Helen Wiltshire. "Unexceptional" was the term that had been uttered a few times throughout her life, by teachers, bosses, parents. Although she always resented being called so, it seemed now to sum it all up pretty accurately. Until *this*, anyway. After *this*, she would be truly exceptional, no matter the outcome.

But would she continue to be Helen Wiltshire? The philosopher in her questioned. She will still have the same consciousness, does that mean the same existence, even if her body is no longer recognisable?

She remembered a time when she was in primary school. Her teacher went around the class asking all the pupils what they wanted to be when they were older. There were all the answers you'd expect: 'Astronaut', 'Spy',

'Zookeeper'. But 9-year old Helen answered, sincerely, "A Pig." Everyone laughed at her, even the teacher, who then said, "Come on now, don't be ridiculous. What do you want to do as a career?" again Helen answered, much to the classes amusement, "Be a Pig." She couldn't think of a profession she was interested in, and still felt this way when she became the age that she was expected to go into one. So, she went into accounting, and hated every minute of it.

"Helen?" A doctor appeared from around the corner. "We've got the document for you, if you would like to have a read." She said before placing the weighty file on the table.

Helen leaned forwards and turned straight to the last page.

And so, she signed away her human rights. She wouldn't need them once it was done.

About the author
Daniel Paton is a young writer who studied Creative Writing at the University of Gloucestershire. He has had short fiction published in anthologies and online journals, and also writes screenplays and stage plays, one of which was performed at Stroud Theatre Festival 2018. He currently lives in Belfast, having just completed his master's degree at Queen's University, where he looks to complete his debut novel.

Transforming Being

Winning entries from the 2019 Waterloo Festival Writing Competition

Introduction

The stories in this collection have come about from a call to submission issued jointly by Bridge House Publishing and the Waterloo Festival. Writers were asked to write a short story or a short monologue on the theme "Transforming Being" in this second year of the Waterloo Festival Writing Competition.

As you will see from this collection there are many interpretations of the theme. We might say that every single one is different. Here are the best eighteen submissions. The others were also very good.

How did we decide on these? We looked for good stories, strong voices and unusual interpretations of the theme. Literary fiction and drama, I'm told, make you think. If you read the last paragraph just after the first you don't get a spoiler. I guess, then, all of these must be quite literary.

We intend to put together a similar e-book in 2020 and also publish all three in a paperback as well in 2020.

It has been a great privilege to work with the Waterloo Festival and with such intriguing writers on this rewarding anthology.

Gill James, editor and partner, Bridge House Publishing, senior lecturer the University of Salford
May 2019

Cat and Mouse

Irene Lofthouse

My Funny Valentine. I love that song. And isn't it a great image, that line about making someone's heart smile? I got warm fuzzies when I saw those words. Never had a Valentine card before. Never had a sweetheart neither, and here I am with a gorgeous bloke wining and dining me, telling me how beautiful and attractive I am. I didn't think at my age I'd have my head turned or be swept off my feet. How wrong could I be? He makes me feel sooo special. He's very attentive and empathetic. I didn't realise men could be like that.

Before I met him, I wasn't really bothered about how I looked, as long as I was neat and tidy for work. Why would I be? No-one was interested in mousy old me. Which is why I was amazed when he asked me out for a drink. He'd called into the library a few times and asked advice, being new to the area. Of course, we all noticed him; a new face does break the monotony, especially one as good-looking as him. Eyes green as spring grass, dark wavy hair, such a melting smile and the grace of cat.

For some reason, we seemed to 'hit it off' as they say, and it wasn't long before we were an 'item'. I could tell that he could see the inner me, the me that was trying to get out, to slough off my mousiness. Empathy you see. Everyone's been amazed at the change in me, especially the hair and clothes. I do feel much better for the weight loss and of course, we look so much better now as a couple. Joel joked about us following the *My Funny Valentine* lyrics; you know, about me being little Miss Mousy, over-looked, ignored. Looking beneath the surface though, Joel saw a work of art, saw the beauty waiting to dazzle.

I wasn't sure of the cosmetic surgery, not at my age, and the price! But I did have the savings, and as Joel pointed out, I should spend it on making me feel good; what else did I have to spend it on? And he was right, I feel fantastic. I am soo looking forward to seeing him.

Joel's a bit squeamish about blood and needles and things, and knowing how much he wants me, and how we can't, not while I'm recovering, we – well I – arranged that he should have a holiday and enjoy himself. He's been so good at sorting the paperwork for the operations, the insurance, the hospital stays, sending me flowers and more, that I think it's only right he should relax. I mean, it wouldn't be much fun looking at me wrapped in bandages. Definitely unphotographable, as the song says. I changed my hair again too. To show that I cared. To show that with my new body, Joel and I would stay together for ever.

Well, he didn't. Stay. Nor did he pay for the operations or insurance. He did manage to clear my bank accounts while I was recovering. And sell my flat. I returned – giddy with excitement and expectation of Joel being there with champagne – to changed locks and confused residents who wouldn't believe I was who I said I was. They showed me a picture that was in the flat when they arrived. One of me with a speech bubble saying "Welcome". I have to admit I understood their confusion. I don't look anything like her now, the woman in the picture.

It took me an age to convince my bank manager too. I had to remind him of books that he'd borrowed, discussions we'd had about favourite authors. Eventually he believed me, becoming profusely apologetic about the circumstances. But the paperwork with my signature authorising the sale of the flat and bank withdrawals was there in black and white. I was penniless.

I decided then, being Miss Mousy no longer, I'd pursue

a different career; one more lucrative than being a librarian. I started that evening. With the bank manager. Freelancing means I've built up some reserves again. And had time to track down my 'sweetheart'. In fact, I'm meeting him tonight. I sent him a Valentine inviting him out for a secret date. I said that I was smitten by his green eyes. That intrigued him. Saw him open the card through his kitchen window. Like I said, I tracked him down. When he opened the card, it played that Police song – the one people think is romantic. You know the one – about breathing, moving, walking. Watching. I've got very good at that. Watching him. Like a cat watches a mouse. This time, I'm the cat.

About the author
Author, storyteller, actor, director, playwright, historian, creative writing tutor, Irene's work covers several genres and ages, appears in many anthologies and canal lock gates. She's appeared at Edinburgh Fringe, in films, on radio and regional theatre. Her plays and books (on Amazon) have toured literature/arts festivals. She's writer in residence with First Story, consultant with Historic England and touring *Words, Women & War*, a one-woman show.

TW: irene_lofthouse

FB: @loftywriter

Climbing Rainbows

Linda Flynn

No-one knew why Dora threw the iron through the window.

Decent, dreamy Dora, in her bland beige clothes, with her pale face that hardly raised a smile, much less flung an iron.

The neighbours could not have been more shocked if a meteorite had landed in their front garden. Their friend Greg laughed that she was stressed, but his wife Tamsin whispered that she was going through The Change. Her husband complained about the cost of the pane and Dora hid the cost of her pain.

The act of extreme ironing requires significant manual dexterity, alongside the thrill of coping with the treacherous mountain terrain. Dora had completed the shirt collar with a flourish and was in the act of abseiling down, when the cuffs became more problematic. A momentary loss of concentration resulted in the iron sliding from her grasp as it followed a curved trajectory down the mountain side.

Next door but one looked at Dora askance. He had once given her a disparaging smirk and informed her that with her lack of presence she would make an excellent spy. Dora found the proposed insult surprisingly appealing and practised melting into shadows, or moulding herself into the corners of rooms, where she would glean all kinds of interesting snippets.

It was when she was laying out the cricket tea that she heard Greg call out to one of his team, "Watch out, big head Ed's coming out to bowl!" The corner of her mouth gave the smallest upward turn as she chopped chunks of cheese.

In a quiet spot by the side of the pavilion, Dora kicked

open her deckchair. She sighed, for her challenge now was to feign interest in the game.

The secret of white-water rafting is to gain maximum momentum whilst steering between rocks without over turning the craft. With buttocks clenched firmly on the inflatable seat, Dora placed one foot hooked under the cross tube and the other braced firmly on the floor. Her arms reached out as she paddled forward, before leaning across and plunging the raft away from hazards.

Later it was assumed that Dora had become too engrossed in Ed's bowling. She was found suspended upside down in her deckchair with her legs poking up in the air, just like one of her sausages on sticks.

To celebrate and prolong his victory, Ed made the benevolent gesture of inviting Greg from the opposing team, with his wife Tamsin to dinner. Dora cooked and Ed opened the wine.

The game was replayed in slow motion, until finally Dora could remove the plates.

"Don't worry, Dora will do the dishes!" called out Ed, flashing a goofy grin, "after all, she's the one who made most of them dirty." Tamsin glanced at the stacked pile of crockery and smiled a faint apology as she slid out of the kitchen.

Dora looked too, at her husband, then at the congealed fat slowly sliding off the cooking tray, before sweeping it up and piling it clattering into the sink. She kicked the door shut on their laughter and the murmur of conversation.

For Dora is a plate spinner and her act requires the deepest concentration. Already she has two plates turning on the draining board, running in rivulets of gravy. She is adding a third, a fourth; can she really keep this going? Dora now has six plates spinning on the side, whilst juggling three more in the air, all of this accompanied to the tune of the Sabre Dance.

71

There was a momentary lapse in conversation when a crash was heard in the kitchen, but no-one left their seat.

The music in Dora's head changed to Zorba the Greek.

The following morning a slight misunderstanding arose. Dora was stripping the duvet cover to go into the laundry basket. Unfortunately, Ed was still asleep in bed.

Dora Grey scarcely noticed, for she was bracing herself to participate in the extreme sport of Blobbing. First she must climb to the highest point, before plunging herself at speed on to the giant air bag, which has someone waiting at the other end to be bounced off. She knows that the higher and heavier her jump, the greater that person will lift off. Let the Blobbing battle begin!

The mattress was replaced fairly quickly, but Ed took a little longer.

About the author

Linda has had two humorous novels published: *Hate at First Bite* for 7 – 9-year-olds and *My Dad's a Drag*, for teenagers. Both won Best First Chapter in The Writers' Billboard competition.

She has six educational books with the *Heinemann Fiction Project*. In addition she has written for a number of newspapers and magazines, including theatre reviews and several articles on dogs.

Linda has had thirteen short stories published in the Bridge House anthologies, Chapeltown CaféLit and from the Waterloo Festival.

Her website is: www.lindaflynn.com.

Disarray

J S Brown

"For years, we crossed the bridge over the long dark mass of water, almost every day," she recalled. "The river running under our feet made our minds wonder, bringing us a sense of possibilities, linking us to the rest of the world."

Contemplative, she remembered a litany of events, especially those inevitable outliers; although the timeline was not irrelevant, her recollection did not strictly follow a chronological sequence, rather, it fell prey to a whimsical popping of memories like white doves out of a magician's colourful silk scarves. Some did not come out at all.

Seagulls

That summer, the seagulls in their scores circled the gardens adjacent to the row of houses near the river, throwing to the air their collective shriek of excitement. That summer they were daring. Was it a new breed that had lost any reticence in approaching people? The child stood valiantly by the rack where soon the burning twigs of thyme and coals would fragrance the meat left on the side, ready to be cooked, not stolen by the rapacious birds. Face covered by her father's safety mask, the child sat next to the coal fire in the garden, tongs in hand, eyes to the sky, ready to fend the birds off.

Still they dived into the small garden, willing to scorch their beaks, their feet, the tips of their wings, at the prospect of the meat laid there in the open. Waving her arms through columns of smoke and shouting, the child sent back the screeching creatures to the banks of the long river. Still they returned, but this time only the smell from the ashes was left.

"Our barbecue is saved!" the child declared.
The blue mass of water flowed, impassibly.

Event Horizon

As was her habit, the happy child skipped her way to school, braving the cold of the morning fog, past the commuters' loud cadenced feet, past some of their grey thoughts that separated them from the pale view from the bridge. Sweeping in tune with her movements, the fringes of the child's scarf danced along each jump, brushing the air with the scent of pink marshmallow. That morning the child stopped to stare at the human form on the edge of a building beside the bridge. She waited for her mother to catch up, then they both stared at the singularity, hand in hand.

"Did it just move?" they asked, puzzled.

Day after day, they witnessed new figures populating the urban horizon around them. More of the rusty humanoid sculptures appeared and, unavoidable, they occupied the bridge; erratic, they loomed out from on top of the roofs. They were happening: surprising at first, expected shortly after, played with later on. That spring, 'count the gormleys' became their favourite game on the way to school, and mornings gained a new dimension.

"Expect the beautiful strange." The mother smiled.

The silver mass of water flowed, impassibly.

Silence I

That day, the capital froze although it was July. Long feared, the unspeakable materialised with the attacks and the city went on lockdown. The mother walked her way over the bridge, her heart out of control, to collect her child kept in school. A time out of time, they walked back together, along with hundreds of fellow pedestrians, adding

74

their own silence to that of the crowd, the multitude of heavy disorientated footsteps on the bridge resonated in unison throughout the city. The seagulls had fled, the traffic was gone. Nothing else stood but the people seeking the brotherhood of the stranger next to them. There would be no trains to take fellow human beings back to their homes that evening, but kindness had found its way, to guide most through their journey.

"This city has welcomed me and my child, it's our home and we are all one," she wept.

The red mass of water flowed, impassibly.

Silence II

That night in June, the city sky reverberated with the thunder of what felt like a thousand storms, ripping apart the heavens with an ancient fear. The lightening erased the orange glow of the city glare, briefly giving a ghostly life to the surrounding buildings in its path.

The skies cleared eventually to give way to the sunrise but little remained as before in the whole land, love washed away.

"Did this town become alien overnight or did I?" she lamented.

Not long after, Ziggy stopped playing guitar for good, setting precedent for a plethora of departing stars.

"Strangers in our own home, disconnected." she said in a muffled voice.

The dark mass of water flowed, impassibly.

Rare Lily

"The skies cleared in the end," she said. Little remained as before; she silenced.

The previous autumn, pale clouds of kamikaze butterflies had come from the garden to die indoors.

Remembering the delicate creatures with no strength left to use their wings, she heard the fortuitous words of a compassionate friend: 'despair is not an option'. She let those five words guide her, like an early star of Bethlehem.

The child, no longer one, made her way across the bridge to join her friends at the march, listening to the radio in her headphones.

"The Radnor lily was spotted this month... it only blooms on an old quarry face in winter... less than one per cent flower..." carried the airwaves.

The gold mass of water flowed, impassibly, forever different, forever the same.

About the author
Born in Lisbon, J S Brown lives in London with her family and enjoys being part of a thriving community in Waterloo. She has recently been developing her painting practice by attending fine art courses at the local Morley College.

Everything Has Changed

Jeanne Davies

We scattered your ashes in your favourite meadow. There were only a few poppies in the hedgerows, so we sprinkled poppy seeds mixed in with you. Like the first smattering of snow it powdered the nettles and wild grasses under the weeping ash tree, making their heads bend in reverence. The breezes will come soon and pick up and dust you into the atmosphere, spreading you far and wide, dancing across the fields we walked in. It will float you into the streams you swam in, where you emerged with your glistening coat, shaking droplets of water multi-coloured with every spectrum of a rainbow.

Everything has changed.

I will try not to look at dead things anymore… at static coloured moths and birds that no longer fly; try not to think of how beautiful they were when they were alive. I must focus my brain away from the pain of those last moments we spent together. Sometimes I feel so alone as I walk, like I'm missing an arm or a leg. But you were so brave, and I know I must be too.

Everything has changed.

The nights are lighter now after suffering many long dark winter nights. You should be running and bobbing up happily through the wheat fields with your ears like errant wings. Always mischievous, always kind-hearted; my loyal best friend and trusted companion. Guardian angel on all our walks, your tail went poker straight upwards when you saw a suspicious person; a sudden warning bark… a cocky swanky walk towards them like your body was formed of rubber. Every day was an adventure we shared; finding pheasants to flush out, or partridges, or even ducks! Your face emerging through the long grasses behind me, running and jumping through the corn, a large toy pheasant held proudly in your soft mouth after a retrieve. I'd whistle you back from chasing deer or that shabby old wily fox that teased you, summoning you to go down flat to the ground when danger lurked. When I had a treat in my hand, you'd prance like a little pony beside me, eyes focused the whole time on mine. They said you were pedigree, named you Moreena Velvet Sunset, and you became a Kennel Club gold awarded dog; but you were just my old Tabitha dog really. Your brilliant hips allowed both hind legs to stretch out behind you like a frog on the carpet, forcing me step over you as I went from room to room. I love you for so many things but mainly the way you've always been beside me… a companion in whatever I did.

Everything has changed.

I stoop as I walk under the apple tree, laden with summer promise. The fruit are only tiny now, but I remember your gleeful early morning face as you spotted a windfall through the glass patio door. I didn't know you wouldn't see the apples ripen this year or get those tufty darts stuck in your fur as the wheat turned to gold. I look for signs of you as I walk through the meadow but there are no new poppies there, just the change of the seasons.

Everything has changed.

It's been nearly five months and the summer has got the urge to go. I've walked alone on many bright summer nights, watching the crimson sunsets lengthen my single shadow across the meadow. I still picture you walking beside me or running ahead after a pheasant. I can still feel the shape of your head when I stroked you and that lovely thick fur you had beneath your neck. I must have vacuumed up every last dog hair of yours from our home now. As the golden hue of autumn approaches, I imagine you galloping through russet leaves as they play ring-oh-the-roses in circles on the ground. My life will be forever autumn now you've gone, with only the early evening moon looking down like a ghost from the sky to keep me company; a crochet doily all alone like me.

Everything has changed.

I wear smarter clothes these days, instead of the dishevelled multi-pocketed jeans splattered with mud and the coat with multiple pockets for treats and poo bags. My walking boots are stored away, pristinely cleaned and polished. My walks are along concrete streets and roads now, going to all the places that you hated; storing those country walks to my cherished memories. I miss them; and I enjoyed being my old scruffy self. Life was so different then.

They say that change is good, and it's true the pain no longer cuts so deep to make my heart bleed. Yet I know that wherever I walk, I'll always be walking with you. I will try not to go back to that dreadful night when you stopped the kitchen clock at 2.50 am to say goodbye... until we meet again dear faithful friend; everything has changed.

About the author
Jeanne Davies has always enjoyed writing fiction and her children grew up with ad-lib stories (sometimes scary!) at bedtime. In recent years more and more of her short stories have been published in anthologies, including some award winning flash fiction and even poetry. One of her stories was recently included in an anthology published in the USA, with another being taken for their next publication.

Havens

Helen Price

Mornings were toughest, joints at their stiffest, pain at its loudest.

Easing plank-like from lying to sitting, aches popped into life in spaces between the pain points, another layer to the insult. Broken body. Sharp intakes of breath, a moment's respite. A sip of water from the glass on the bedside locker, a distraction if nothing else. More deep breaths, then reaching into the locker and a clumsy grabbing of the pill packs, thumb-push from behind and satisfying crackles as each tablet broke from its sealed silver confinement and he threw the triple multi-coloured dose down his throat. More water and an 'ahhhh'.

He wondered sometimes if the worst of his pain was arthritis or from the injury. The doctor said he might have developed arthritis anyway but the injury had just exacerbated it. Well, what did it matter – pain was pain. He waited for the drug-effect to stream through his veins and soak the nerves to balm his senses and finally he was able to get up, released from the worst of it, for now at least. He walked to the bathroom, stick in hand, slowly.

Years ago this house had had other occupants – his mother and father. He'd never married. He'd meant to, vaguely and there had once been Jean, so distant now. The looking after of his parents had got in the way. That's probably what happened, he mused, if he thought about it. There was no way he'd have let them go into a home just like there was no way he was going to a home. Funny, the name 'home' when really it was nothing like one, more a housing place full of people you didn't want to be with and all the time your own home was there, willing you to stay.

80

Well, he was *going* to stay. At home. But his parents had had him to keep them. Who would keep him? Would he be able to stay? Would 'they' make him go?

He looked through the bathroom window as he shaved. Lucky, he considered himself, in having so much green space, a field more than a garden, fenced off, wild. He was unable to tend it much anymore, unable to afford a gardener and happy, really, with the wilderness. Only yesterday he'd seen a hedgehog, spines glinting in the sun, snout-nose twitching, waddling across the grass as if bent on a mission and it had brought a smile to his face. What was it up to? Where was it going? The little creatures were common when he was young, a rare sight now. He'd followed it with his eyes from his seated position on the patio until it disappeared under a bush. He scanned now, hoping to catch a glimpse of it again but no sighting.

The doorbell's shrill ring made him jump and he sighed. The carer. Bath day. The one-a-week. Well, at least he was ahead of her, shave done – important to keep up with his little successful demonstrations of independence.

"Hel-lo Eddie, only me-ee," she called in sing-song as she let herself in.

"Hello there, Rosie," he said, shuffling into the hallway, "I've just had my shave."

"Well done," she said, getting close and peering at his face. "And a good one it is, too."

He'd passed the test.

Chit-chat and toing-and froing, a big blue bath towel pulled from the cupboard, toiletries placed on the edge of the bath and the taps turned on full. Rosie matched the flow of the water with a flow of her own about her boss and her last client and his cancer and her daughter's boyfriend and what a waster he was and Emma could do better and her upcoming days off and her hair and how she was thinking of changing the colour again, clattering around all the while so that it would have been difficult to hear even if he'd wanted.

He didn't mind her chatter – he liked it, in fact, even if his mind was wandering, all the time thinking, 'she's not the type to give me a bad report.'

Bath-chair and submerging and shampoo and bubbles and scents and splashing and ten minutes later he emerged scrubbed and fresh and, he had to admit, energised. Sitting in his chair with a welcome cuppa in the kitchen he watched Rosie continue her work, wiping, putting away things, still talking.

"I'm thinking of going out later," he said. "On my scooter." More evidence.

"Good for you, Eddie!" she replied. "Take care on those uneven paths now, won't you."

When she'd gone he bumbled around for longer than he'd care to admit, gathering, checking, re-arranging, trying to remember simple things he'd need, shopping bags, his keys, the phone he barely knew how to use, so much to think of so that he wouldn't have to turn back. Finally outside, he felt drawn to the garden. He walked, looking around, though he was unsure what for. Stick in hand he kept going, past the roses, the wisteria, all the tough perennials and bushes that required little attention, past the untended vegetable patch, full of weeds now where once, under his care, there had been neat rows of carrots and onions and potatoes. On he went, less aware of his stiffness; he hadn't been down this far for a long time and at last he was at the end, in front of the Hillman Hunter, rusted, crumpled, wheels deflated like diseased lungs, lying obscenely tilted on its side, windows cracked and covered in moss. He peered inside through the permanently half-open passenger door simultaneously expectantly gawping and welcoming.

He'd sustained his injuries in it but could never get rid of a beloved object. And now the hedgehog had made a home in it. *Ahhh!*

Revived, looser, limbering up and straightening up, he headed back, stick more ornament than functional now. A weight lifted, he knew he was going to stay. Right here.

About the author
Helen Price lives in Bristol and works full-time as a nurse for the ambulance service. She has written three novels but mostly writes short stories nowadays. Drawing on a long history in nursing, health is one of her major themes but she's also inspired by environmental and social issues. She has had her short stories published regularly in *Scribble* magazine.

Heat

Amelia Brown

I wake up dreaming of you and cannot get back to sleep. My hands are sweating. The noise of the television is coming up through the floor like steam. Someone is a winning a football game. Someone else is losing.

A slight breeze grazes the tips of my nipples. It's sometime in the afternoon and the heat beats like global warming has been accelerated. The sky is the colour of streetlamps. It makes the ceiling look like skin.

I pad downstairs and watch the back of you. You are wearing a jumper I have only seen before on your father and it grazes thighs that I like best around my neck.

"Sit outside," you say. "Heat's pelting." You don't turn around.

I sit on the patio in my underwear. The graze of stone against my skin is a welcome erosion. The moon is out already, hanging low and nearly pink.

"She feels nice, yeah? That sun?" I can't see you inside. I wait for your hands on my shoulders but they don't come.

"It's just water but it's cold. You'll feel it. I never knew how cold water going through your body could feel until this. Like a snake."

Now your hands come and they stick to my shoulders like plastic. I shrug them away. You're right about the water, though – the way it slips through me, I've never felt anything like it.

The air between us feels thick like one of us could choke on it. I imagine you choking. I imagine saving you. Then I imagine watching it happen and doing nothing except continuing to sip the snake water.

"We could fuck if you want," you say, biting yellow nail varnish off your fingers.

"Do you want to?"

"It passes the time. It's dragging, isn't it? Isn't it? You feel it too."

I hold the glass to my forehead. "Yeah why not. Let's fuck."

We fuck on the rug in the living room until our thighs burn. Afterwards you take a shower and I wash myself from the kitchen sink. Out of the window I can see the world melting.

You come downstairs and you kiss my elbow and you say, "That was hot."

"Do you still love me?"

You walk over to the patio doors and lean your head against the glass. "The world's melting," you say. "Did you notice?"

"Yes."

"No." You don't look at me as you say this which is how I know what the no refers to.

"Water?" I ask. I turn the tap until the water is pouring out as wide as my wrist and the sound of it is pounding like falling trees. Through the window I watch the sky begin to bend towards us like it is finally giving in to an illicit love affair with our roof tiles.

"No," you say again.

"I heard you."

"Why didn't you say anything?"

It's an awful situation, isn't it? To know that your lover doesn't love you and also that the world is ending. The ground is beginning to fizz. That's something I'm certain I can hear. No, the ground is beginning to rumble. That's something I'm certain I can feel in my toes.

"You ought to say something," you say like you are spitting the words out your mouth.

Then the windows go orange.

"What's happened?" you scream, and I feel your body running to mine.

"The sun probably exploded," I say, trying not to cry because your hands are clinging to my shoulder blades.

Gradually the light clears. Everything we own, or have owned up until this moment, is covered in pieces of the sky. You don't let go of my hand.

"Look," you say, and point upwards. Through a tear in the atmosphere, we can see this seething blackness. "Is that the universe?"

I am thinking about your hand. I am thinking that your palms are softer than the lips of God. I am thinking that maybe another explosion will fuse our hands together. Or maybe I will refuse to let go.

"Come on," you say. And because you are holding my hand I follow. We climb through the roof, over the sky and onto the atmosphere which feels like the skin of a balloon stretched over a burning core.

We sit on the edge of the atmosphere and dangle our feet over Earth.

"When this is over, will you leave me?" I ask.

"Will it ever be over?"

"That isn't the question."

You lean my head into your neck like I am child.

"Every time I look at the stars I'll think of you. Every time I see the sky I'll think of you. Every time it is warm. Every time I drink water. Even if I didn't leave, I wouldn't be able to love you."

The next morning I wake up in a bed and you aren't there and the sky is white and the air is cold as the Arctic. The moon is still lingering, hanging low outside my window.

"At least it's over," she says, and winks at me. I curl back into a caterpillar sleep and wait for my cocoon to form.

86

About the author

Amelia is an emerging writer living in London. She is a member of the Roundhouse Poetry Collective 2018/19 and is on the John Burgess Playwriting Course 2018/19. She is currently working on her debut novel which was shortlisted for the Penguin WriteNow Mentorship Programme 2018/19.

Old Masters

Beverley Byrne

As a fellow art historian, you'll appreciate the importance of the artist's signature. Actually, I have two. Working swiftly, my final flourish is minimalist in style whilst languorous masterpieces deserve a more elaborate mark. If you like, I can show you my past accomplishments. I have photographs. Dozens of them. But in the meantime, I bet you're dying to know how it started.

Picture me, if you will, a little girl on an underground platform with her mother. Studying Old Masters taught me about myths and legends, but as an ignorant infant, I had only my imagination. Subterranean dragons lurked in a sooty abyss where invisible agonised souls screeched and rattled their chains. That journey into the maul of darkness was terrifying. Since then, I've never really cared for trains, although occasionally they have, over the course of my career, served a purpose.

It wasn't until years later I discovered the truth behind that memory. I always wondered why mother didn't come back to save me from that dingy terraced house in Ilford. After all, she'd promised. I was fifteen when my father, in one of his snivelling, post coital bouts of self-loathing, put me straight. The snorting dragon swallowed my mother the day she delivered me into hell. I thought about asking Granny if this were true. But why bother? Look what happened when I tried to tell her about father. She just turned her stooped back to me and delivered one of her sermons. Being clever would deliver me from evil she repeated, fingering the crucifix at her throat. That much was true.

The summer after my first year at Magdalen, I travelled

to Paris to study the great masters in the Louvre. The Wreck of the Medusa unlocked something in me. Gericault did not simply paint suffering, he'd done his homework. Visiting hospitals and morgues, he studied the colour and hue of dead and dying flesh. Gericault's genius catapulted me into an obsession with tone and pigment, shade and chiaroscuro. It wasn't the depiction of death so much as rendering it tangible that intrigued me. Once I'd got my eye in, there was no stopping me. I roamed the world gobbling up artistic technique in two dimensions. You know the rest of course. After all, it was you who supervised my doctorate.

What you don't know, since by then you'd moved on to another impressionable Royal College graduate, was how my academic achievements dovetailed with my hobby. Being obsessed by surfaces, I naturally gravitated towards cinema. It was the same thing really. How did they create those celluloid faces? What secrets transformed a winsome ingenue into an old hag, the chiselled screen idol into a disfigured war veteran? With cosmetics, wigs and prosthetics, time elapsed and fresh identities emerged. I attacked the art of make up with the same lust for perfection which characterised my passion for painting.

I wasn't just good, I was brilliant. After the initial course, I interned with production companies who adored me. Within a few years, I'd been headhunted by Hollywood. You have no idea how useful this has been to my art. For a start, travelling the world to far off film locations makes detection difficult. Murder scenes in Tokyo tend to not to flag up in the suburbs of Toronto. And, as by now you will have realised, I am an Oscar winner in the art of disguise. This is why when I'm captured on CCTV in Patagonia or Portugal, the same person never appears twice. Male or female, old and young, I like to challenge myself. It makes the denouement so much more rewarding. There's nothing like seeing a grainy picture or photofit of yourself being someone else on television or newspapers across the globe. The sense of omnipotent power is breathtaking.

I expect you'd like to know how I choose my subjects. Generally, I go for bores, braggarts and those who deceive and demean women. The first two attributes are optional but the last two are essential. Like Gericault, research is the key to success. When I have time, I really get to know them; make sure I'm doing society a favour. I have my standards to uphold. That's why, when possible, I never select the father of young children. That would be too cruel.

As you will by now appreciate, I prefer my subjects to know why and what will happen. My favoured modus operandi involves ketamine and a long, sharp, decorative hat pin – a memento from a happy time working on Scorsese's Edith Wharton. On other occasions, and this is where the trains come in, some braying lout attracts my attention. How easy it is when the platform is crammed with high spirited party people, to produce the cattle prod from my designer handbag and give the moron a fatal nudge just as the train thunders in. Naturally, I can't do this too often but diversification can be gratifying.

I know what you're wondering. Why wait so long for you? It's been years, hasn't it? Well, the best is always worth waiting for and you were the reason I started my hobby. I didn't realise it at the time but there were aspects of you which reminded me of father. A monster at heart, he was good at disguising it. The boyish charm, effortless wit, the expensive gifts. And he loved me. In these respects, you could have been twins.

My feral father never had your education but he was wily. In a different and infinitely more intelligent fashion, you beguiled and abused me so I hung on your every word

90

and waited for your phone call. You didn't notice but towards the end, I emulated you. I adopted your adorable lisp, your habit of wearing dungarees and the strawberry scent you favoured. Daft really. Looking at you now, you're the last person I'd want to be.

About the author
Beverley Byrne is a freelance journalist specialising in travel, celebrity profiles and interiors for a range of national magazines and newspapers. Previously a lecturer in film history at London University, she exchanged academia for travel writing after being commissioned to cross the Atlantic Ocean on a banana boat bound for the Caribbean. She lives in London.

Over the Wall

Paula R C Readman

"It's a sell-out, but I'm sure we'll find a way in," Jamie said, peering round the corner, his back pressed against the wall, his elbows scraping the dusty red bricks.

At twelve, he stood in his usual attire of grimy black shorts, faded grey T-shirt, and with his matchstick legs pushed into tatty plimsolls.

From the other side of the wall, amid the hustle and bustle of roadies shouting, echoes of familiar pieces of music floated on the light summer breeze as the band tuned their instruments.

"Come on," I yelled.

In the summer's heat, I'm as restless as the crowd that milled about waiting for the gates to open. "Let's do something else," I moaned, wiping beads of sweat from my forehead.

It was Jamie's idea to gate-crash the open-air concert in our local park. I was more than happy to sit by the river fishing while listening to their latest hits.

"Ajay, you can be such a bore at times. It's a chance to meet someone famous," Jamie said trying to persuade me to join him in his endeavours.

I sighed heavily and looked over at the reeds where we'd hidden our fishing gear at the water's edge. I'd argued with him that my mother wouldn't allow me to spend money on seeing a rock band, but I knew as soon as the words had left my mouth, I'd already lost the argument.

"You won't need to ask your mum for money. I'll get us in," Jamie said.

When it came to Jamie's heart desire, he was full of bright ideas. If he wanted something, he would always find a means of getting it.

My mum said Jamie's family were as poor as church mice, whatever that meant. His mum was hard working, like my parents, but I knew nothing about his father, nor I'm sure did Jamie. I enjoyed his company. To our classmates, we made an odd couple, both outsiders, but I guessed that's what drew us together.

Originally, my family came from India. Jamie's from Scotland. We both carried traces of our ancestry in the tones of our voices and our skin colouring. Me with my jet-black hair, thin brown limbs while Jamie sported shocking red hair and creamy pale skin. Across the bridge of his nose, a wave of ginger freckles became more visible in the summer while my skin darkened.

Jamie's blue eyes narrowed as he stepped away from the wall, not bothering to brush his elbows. "Come on, Ajay. Let's try somewhere else."

He moved on bony legs, his undernourished body visible through his T-shirt. His knees bearing scabby scars from other battles, with walls, trees and anything he could climb to look over. No barrier was too high for him, and I was happy to follow.

My mother always fed him when he came to our house and Jamie would never decline bowls of rice and butter chicken.

The first time Jamie lifted a bowl to lick up every speck of gravy, I tried to tell him not to, but my mother silenced me with her stare.

"He's such a good lad," she told me in Punjabi as we sat in our kitchen.

"What's your Mum saying?" Jamie asked.

"She likes you." I said as Mother beamed her beautiful smile.

"Tell her, I love her cooking. I don't get anything like it at home. Mum's always busy."

My mum nodded, understanding more than she lets on. It's her safety net in a tough world, not laziness as some believed.

I followed Jamie along the footpath that ran between the river and the wall. Here no one guarded it, but thistles and stinging nettles.

In the industrial days of Britain, during the building of its empire, the footpath was once known as 'a towpath' according to my father, used by horses pulling the narrow boats of coal from the coalmines to the factories. In those days, the waterways were the highways across the country before railways.

Finally, we reached a bend in the wall where a massive oak tree stood. I saw the all too familiar look crossing Jamie's face that told me the tree had set him a challenge. Its huge branches spread like welcoming arms to him as it towered over us.

I closed my eyes, and offered up a prayer to any Gods hoping that at least one of them was listening. As Jamie circled the tree trunk, he reminded me of Jack with the beanstalk from a Christmas panto my father had taken us to see.

"You can't climb it, Jamie," I called over the stinging nettles.

"Just watch me, Ajay," he yelled, pressing his back against the wall and his feet against the tree trunk. Slowly, he inched his way up like Spiderman to the top of the wall until he was sitting on it. "Come on, Ajay, I'll give you a hand up."

I'm not sure what happened next. One minute Jamie, with his shocking red hair, was standing there all smiles, the next he wasn't. Like Jack who disappeared into the clouds at the top of the beanstalk, he was gone.

I shouted to him, but I heard nothing, just the music and crowds clapping in time to the heavy beat.

As I stand here years later, a man now, I can't believe, Jamie climbed so high. The wall's still standing, but the tree has gone.

"Ajay, my old friend, your mum said you'd be down here fishing. Good job they paved the footpath otherwise I'd never have got my wheels down to join you."

"Good to see you, Jamie. You're looking well."

"All the fresh air and travelling."

"It suits you."

"You know me, Ajay. Never one for putting barriers in my way, just have to make sure my brake is on, as I know you can't swim."

I laughed. Casting out before handing Jamie the fishing rod, suddenly his disability has gone, and we're laughing like kids again in the afternoon sunshine.

About the Author

Paula R. C. Readman's first success was when English Heritage selected her story for publication. Since then she had 20 short stories published and won two competition including the Harrogate Crime writing Festival/ Writing Magazine competition when crime writer, Mark Billingham selected her story *Roofscapes* as the overall winner.

Find out more about Paula and her writing on her Amazon Author page, or on her blog:
http://paulareadman1.wordpress.com

Russian Doll

Jessica Joy

Every morning, in the mirror, I practice empathy. I stare at myself. I turn sideways and smooth the pressed pleats of my uniform over the rounded bump of my baby. My freshly laundered tunic still smells of antiseptic. I pin back my hair, adjust my watch, and check my pockets for pens and scissors. I still have Mrs Parker's wristband which I removed when we signed her over to the mortuary, yesterday. I smile. I am a good nurse.

If I were a Russian doll, this outfit, this 'character' would be the last section before the little solid piece in the middle.

Today, at work, I will speak with Mrs Parker's family. Practical, dependable, efficient nurse will be insufficient. Today, I will need to adopt another face. She is the kind, nurturing carer that I bring out for bereaved families. I will allay their fears, pat their hands, and assure them that their relative passed quickly and peacefully. I will make a good mother.

Later, to celebrate another week over, it's the work's outing. I look forward to putting on a different layer. This one keeps colleagues guessing; hair down, bright lipstick, short skirt. This little Russian doll knows how to have a good time. But no vodka. I need to keep a clear head. I cannot afford any slip-ups; any loose, alcohol-fuelled confessions.

Tomorrow is Sunday best. The outer most section of my Russian doll; shiny, painted, demure, head scarf and smock dress, God-fearing. Although, I have abandoned God; I have my own plan now.

Each shell covers the one beneath and hidden, deep

inside them all, is the solid kernel of truth. This is the still, small voice that encouraged me as I stroked Mrs Parker's cheek and dabbed her dry lips with moist cotton wool. The small voice that praised my benevolence as I injected the liquid into the old lady's IV line. The small voice that gave me strength to hold the old woman still as she shuddered her last breath.

I can take apart the garish husks, the costumes, the glossy, lacquered facades of my life, because safe in the centre is my one true self; I am the angel of mercy.

About the author

Jessica writes from the family home in Deal.

Her play *Full Circle* was performed for the Greenwich Arts Festival in 1991. She has several short stories published in anthologies including "Graduation" in *With Our Eyes Open* (published by Curtis Bausse).

When not writing, Jessica enjoys spending time with her family, including the dog, and tap dancing. Sometimes all at the same time.

Steam

Sinéad Kennedy Krebs

"You have no choice."

For the first time in her life, Ada turned her head to stare through the grille. She could make out few features of the shadowy figure sealing her fate. His voice was solemn, condemning; a voice that could only act as a mouthpiece for God. She barely listened to it as he gave her penance, and absolved her of a sin she had not yet committed.

"Amen," they murmured in unison.

"We must all make our sacrifices in times like these," he said, as she got up to leave. She left the comment hanging in the air, slipping slightly on the tiled floor, worn smooth by thousands of fearful feet.

There was ice in the wind that cut to her spine. Wrapping her shawl closer around her as she walked to the house, she looked up at the blueish shadow of the mountains, cursing those hiding there. She heaved the old blue door and went to the kitchen, lifting a kettle of water onto the stove. As the steam began to rise, she locked the door and pulled out the copper bath.

Ada breathed in her husband's chest, still moss, mountain and salt despite the hot bath she'd given him. He smelled different. He was different. The past seven months were written into the new lines on his face, the sandpaper roughness of his hands, the grey of his eyes. She didn't know how long Tom would be home, or how long until he'd be home again. She didn't know if he would be home again at all. She curled into him, tucking her dark hair under his chin, tracing his skin with long fingers.

"I never want to get up again." She smiled, shouts from the children in the street outside reminding her that she'd have to, sooner or later. Tom pulled her in closer, pressing his mouth to the top of her head, closing his eyes. They stayed like that, tightly, listening to the games outside.

The pale gloom of the early evening slunk through the lace in the window, turning the white sheets grey. Ada twisted out of her husband's arms and began to dress herself, pinning her hair back to go out and call to the children. She ran a warm hand through Tom's rust-coloured hair, holding his face. He kissed her palm, inhaling the Lily of the Valley on her wrist.

An urgent banging stopped them dead. Running to the window, Ada saw the cluster of familiar uniforms in the street, the children lined up against the wall, eyes down. Wordlessly, she turned back to her husband, who was already half dressed.

"I'll go down then," she whispered. "I can stop them for only a minute."

He nodded, and leant over to kiss her. She looked back at him from the door for what she knew could be the last time. In the half-light, he looked like a ghost.

A trail of steam rose from the stream of tea. Mrs Mulligan passed a cup to Ada and kept the cracked one for herself, holding the handle awkwardly to hide the spidery fissure through the china. They pursed their lips as they sipped silently, keeping the leaves at bay.

"You have him off the breast then?" Mrs Mulligan nodded towards the door, where James was asleep outside in his pram.

"I have."

"Good, so. Sooner he's onto solids, sooner he'll grow. Another lovely little lad."

He was. Sturdy, red cheeked and red haired. The women of the town had breathed a sigh of relief when he was born; this baby, with his fat hands and bellowing cries, was a baby that would live.

Ada slid her cup over the table. She'd been drinking tea with Mrs Mulligan since before that was her name, when they were still in pinafores, telling made-up fortunes of romance and adventure. They'd been in trouble for using the sugar, the tannin too bitter. Now they were women who wasted nothing, carefully measuring their sugar, their tea leaves, their words.

Mrs Mulligan tilted the cup.

"Now," she said, contemplating the arrow in the leaves. "Mr Mulligan was papering the Hennessey offices last week."

"The lawyers?"

"Yes. He overheard something about a list." She didn't look up from the dregs. "Tom's name is on that list."

Ada stood up, gathering her shawl around her. Her friend caught her hand and squeezed. The women nodded together, and Ada went out.

They pushed past before she could properly open the door, flooding the house like a burst pipe. She ran to the stairs, blocking their way and attempting haughtiness.

"I demand to know what it is you're doing in my house again."

A rifle butt to her ribs made her collapse into the bannister, splitting her lip. Soldiers in mismatched uniforms ran up past her, tearing apart the quiet of the evening with aggressive foreign accents. She was marched into the kitchen where the copper bath stood in the corner, cold now. Only a few hours ago Tom had lurked in the doorway, a half smile on his weather-beaten face and the stink of seven months in his suit. A crash upstairs told her they'd found no trace. He was gone.

Ada inhaled the rising steam as it fogged up the window, filling the bath kettle by kettle until she could submerge herself entirely. She pulled the whiskey from where her husband hid the bottle, watching the steam rise and curl, the copper shimmering in the failing light. The whiskey stung her still healing lip as she sipped, savouring the flavour, the pain, the cleansing and sanctifying burn.

She dropped her gaze to her belly, still flat underneath the boning. Tom had been home a matter of hours, leaving her with another open mouth and nothing to feed it with but rebellion.

The water in the bath was scalding. Ada whispered the words of Father Murphy.

"We must all make our sacrifices in times like these."

About the author

Sinéad Kennedy Krebs is a writer, former actor, and academic, currently researching a PhD in English Literature at King's College London, exploring the cultural legacies of the First World War in Ireland. Sinéad is a member of the Marketing team at Morley College London, and co-host of forthcoming podcast series The Imposters Club.

sineadkk.wordpress.com

Take Your Place

Gail Aldwin

It will be Christmas lunch at my sister's again. She thinks there's nowhere else for me to go and that I'm helpful in the kitchen. Her daughters always spend Christmas at home and my nephew is coming with his wife for the first time. Including the grandchildren, we are thirteen in total. This displeases my sister who is somewhat superstitious. Leave an empty chair at the end of the table, she tells me, no one will need to sit there but at least we won't be an odd number. That'll look strange, comes my response, but I have an idea. Dressing the Christmas table is my responsibility, so I'll lay an extra place, you know, for the sake of symmetry. She repeats the word symmetry and nods in agreement. What have you planned for the centrepiece? she asks.

Although I'm expected to sit near my sister, I change the place cards so I'm seated at the other end, next to the carver with its sturdy armrests. She gives me one of her stares but I'm too far away to feel the effect. My sister can't have everything her own way and besides, I have you to think about. I've laid your place setting carefully, the knife blade turned inwards and your linen napkin is folded into a crown. I watch you tap the prongs on your fork then you drum a tune with your thumb on the edge of your plate. I curl my fingers into yours and you grip my hand tightly. Tilting my head, I see there are wisps of grey in your fringe and the laughter lines around your eyes have deepened. After a decade as a widow, I'm pleased to sit beside you at the top of the table once more.

About the author

Gail Aldwin is an award-winning writer of fiction and poetry. Her work includes *The String Games,* a contemporary novel (Victorina Press, 2019) *adversaries/comrades*, a poetry pamphlet (Wordsmith_HQ, 2019) and *Paisley Shirt* (Chapeltown Books, 2018) which was long listed in the best short story category of the Saboteur Awards 2018. Gail co-writes short plays and comedy sketches that have been staged in Bridport, Brighton and Salisbury.

Twitter: @gailaldwin

Blog: https://gailaldwin.com

The Father-Daughter Club

Yvonne Walus

The first rule of the Father-Daughter Club is: you talk about the daughter. All the time.

"How can I help you today?" The sales girl at the cosmetics store is bubbly, her expression totally focused on me.

I use my opening smile, the baffled-and-slightly-embarrassed one. "It's my daughter's birthday this weekend and I'd like to buy her…" I trail off.

"Wow, happy birthday to your daughter! How old?"

The conversation flows easily, and soon my shopping basket is filled with citrus-scented soaps, coffee body scrubs and bath bombs guaranteed to turn the water into liquid gold. I even buy a natural shampoo bar that doesn't need a plastic bottle ("so environmentally-friendly!") and chocolate-flavoured lip balm ("teenagers love it!").

"Can you gift-wrap each item separately? My daughter loves opening presents."

I pay cash, asking for change in ten-dollar notes, and walk out of the shop with a spring in my step and the sales girl's contact details in my phone. Friday lunchtime well spent.

On the way to the office, I pass four homeless men, and I give them each a tenner. Ten bucks will buy two coffees, or two big burgers with fries, or a hit of whatever they need to make their lives bearable for a few hours. Who am I to judge?

That evening, I kick off my shoes and pull off the necktie.

"I'm home," I call out, though I don't expect an answer. Sprawled on the sofa, I dial one of the numbers in my Star Contacts. "A pepperoni pizza for me, and a vegetarian one

104

for my daughter," I tell the guy who picks up the phone at the local shop.

The wine bottle opened to breathe and the bath products put away in the cupboard, I browse the movie options while waiting for dinner to be delivered to my doorstep. This is the good life. If my daughter were here, we'd probably argue about which show to watch, so it's just as well that I'm alone.

I invented my daughter fifteen years ago. My first job, a few months in, I got asked to work over the long weekend. Normally, I would have agreed, but I'd already booked a romantic get-away. My then-girlfriend was going hot and cold on me, and I needed the opportunity to figure out what's what. Using an engagement ring, no less.

Plus, the project was super-boring.

"I'm so sorry," I said, pulling my mouth into a disappointed grin. "Would love to, but I need to look after my baby daughter. Her mum," I broke off, mumbled something. "Anyway, she's out of the picture for now. And my parents live in England." That last bit at least was true.

"Oh, wow. I didn't realise you're a solo dad," my boss touched my shoulder, the briefest of contacts, but a major barrier broken. "You should have mentioned it."

If I were a mother, a woman who tried to use her child as a reason not to work on a Saturday, I would have been deemed less-than-professional and not fully committed to my career. A man, though – what a bloke!

Unfair, I know. I felt bad. Then I felt even worse when I got dumped while on one knee holding up a diamond ring. Thinking back, perhaps it was karma. Or maybe Abigail – the only woman who'd ever made me want to settle down – simply wasn't that into me.

The feeling of guilt at the office was amplified when I

got promoted to a team leader position, because – as a father – I'd be a good fit for the role. The irony being, not many mothers hear that their parenting skills make them a natural manager.

So yes, it's all super-unfair and super-unethical. But to paraphrase a great modern philosopher, we are all slaves with white collars chasing after cars and clothes, working jobs we hate so we can buy stuff we don't need. Think about today's jobs – not nurses and builders – but all the middle managers and senior managers, the data crunchers and advertisers. How many of them could disappear tomorrow, leaving the fabric of our society intact? My own self included.

Saturday night, the gift-wrapped shampoo bar in hand, I arrive at my current girlfriend's apartment. "Happy one-month anniversary," I tell her as I hand her the present.

Tanya is an environment fanatic, so the idea of shampoo without a plastic bottle is an instant hit. We are consumers. No matter how careful Tanya may be about plastics, she's still into material things.

"You must be exhausted after the whole day of child-minding," Tanya says. She thinks my daughter is five. "Tell you what. Instead of going out, why don't I whip up a Thai omelette, while you relax and watch TV?"

I pull her close. "Sounds like heaven." It's the truth. I love home-cooked meals, but it's always too much bother to prepare dinner for one. "Forget the TV, though. Let's talk."

TV I get enough of at home. The main reason I date is for the company for another human being.

Lame? You bet.

"Can you stay till morning?" Tanya asks after we've eaten.

It's good to wake up with someone I like. Unfortunately,

I don't like Tanya that much. "Sorry… The babysitter needs to go home at midnight."

"We'd better hurry up, then," she says as she dims the lights.

As soon as I get home the next evening, the doorbell rings. A young person is standing on my doormat. Short hair with a purple fringe that covers most of the face. A gold stud in the nose, like a pimple full of pus ready to be squeezed. Laddered jeans, one hole so big you can see the knee.

It looks up at me. Female. Something familiar around the jawline. Eyes the exact replica of Abigail's, hard like the diamond I tried to give her all those years ago.

The girl swings her backpack into my limp arms.

"Hi dad," she says.

About the author
When Yvonne Walus is not a novelist, she's a Doctor of Mathematics. A Business Analyst. A wife and a mother. A cat slave. And always, always a writer. Her crime novel series is set in South Africa, and she also has a new thriller series set in New Zealand. Please visit www.yvonnewalus.com for more information.

The Professional

Allison Symes

I should've been a salesman. I have a way with words. Put "unique" and "opportunity" in an advert and you hook in the gullible, who don't question why they might be the ideal ones for this chance, which strangely had never occurred before. Why they never query that is beyond me but it's useful. I suspect every con artist has thought that.

I can take my pick. My bosses have given me leeway, which is great. I've not let them down either. Given them all they wanted. Was praised at my last review too. I was told whatever I was doing was working so I should stick at it. Fair enough. Not going to argue with that. Had a pay rise last month too, which the lovely missus and I spent on slap up meals. Loved that.

It is all on the quota system of course. The more I can get to hook up to my special offer, the more commission I get but, hey, I'm a being of the world and these schemes go on everywhere. Okay, most of these sales things don't involve abducting alien beings and taking them back to my home planet where they will be transformed from what they were to, well, meat when all is said and done, but hey I'm just doing my job and we've all got to live…

See, my planet ran out of sources of protein ages ago. We polluted the world and killed off our wildlife. Okay, we built ourselves a dome which sustains life but it has done sod all to get our animals back so we have to look for meat elsewhere. Having survived a pollution nightmare, we're not going to let ourselves starve, are we? Come on, you'd do the same.

Now where I am this week? Oh yes. The bosses want me to go back to Earth again. So Earth it is then, which is one of my easier markets. Humans are so open to being able to make money out of doing very little so I exploit that greed and laziness. The nice thing is they don't get away with it. By the time they realise they're never seeing their home planet again, it is far too late to do anything. I think there's a kind of justice here. I'm taking the useless layabouts away from Earth too. Just give me time. Even I can't clear them all in a week or so. I'll need years I suspect! Still, it is good to know I won't run out of supplies. The professional always makes sure of that.

Oh and before you ask, I don't do the transformation into meat bit. That's Robot 918's job. We use robots for the grotty tasks. Saves me hearing the screams too. Gets in the way of doing the job having to hear that so I don't. Got to be professional, haven't I? Do the job, no hard feelings and all that, but just get it done and on to the next one. It's a shame really. I've studied Earth and humanity. I see humans used machines for rotten jobs too. We have so much in common. It's just a pity one of our species has to be the predator and the other the prey. There's no way my lot are being the latter so bad luck to you.

If you want to protect yourself from what is out there, and trust me there are stranger species than mine out in the big, bad universes, don't fall for the con tricks. I shouldn't be telling you this really but I've always had a soft spot for those who make the best of what they've got and work hard. I know some of you do that.

My bosses don't care who I pick to bring back but I do. I see it as part of my journey to being accepted as professional by those above me in the old hierarchy. Some look down on me because of my lowly background. Can't be having with that so working hard and seeing things through is the only way to convince my lot I can make something of myself. And I am getting there, as the pay rise proves! I also see it as the difference between being a mere amateur who does his job for the money and perks and being the professional who cares about what he does. I'm sure the meat, sorry transformed being if you prefer, tastes better for it too.

Time to be off again then. I've got nice transport too. A flick of a few buttons and I'm whizzing through space as if there was nothing to it. I don't understand all the technology I admit but when I think my dear old dad was a slave and had to clear out the pollution mines, I can't help but feel he'd be proud of me. He died young of course. There's a limit to how much pollution anyone can stand but I won't die young. Dad would be proud of me for bettering myself. I'm bringing the family up the social ladder so we're transforming too. The missus is proud of me and yes I get bulk packs of meat as part of my pay so it's win-win.

Now where shall I go this time? Oh yes, one of those small places I think. Set the co-ordinates to the United Kingdom. Let's go and hook in the punters. I've got promises and orders to deliver and I am a being of my word, always. It's what professionals *do*.

And I never let down the customers. They are always right after all.

About the author

Allison Symes is published by Chapeltown Books, Cafélit, and Bridge House Publishing amongst others. She is a member of the Society of Authors and Association of Christian Writers. Her website is www.allisonsymescollectedworks.wordpress.com and she blogs for Chandler's Ford Today: http://chandlersfordtoday.co.uk/author/allison-symes/.

This Side Of Blue:

Christopher Bowles

I remember who I was before I met you; but only in shades of grey.

My every childhood memory is a black and white frame in a slide-show; a sepia photograph full of muted browns and charcoal shadows. I see pictures of happy families. Birthday parties on garden patios, first swimming lessons, and get-togethers in church halls. But they all lack colour.

I once heard that people only dream in black and white. Only 'true artists' dream in living Technicolor. (So back then, I guess I was still in Kansas, Toto.) And the day we met, I was changed. The tornado came, blew me over the rainbow, and I was suddenly someone different. I was loved. And I loved.

I loved you.

Do you remember how we first met? It should have been a story straight from the silver screen. I walk into a jazz club, and see you singing on stage and our eyes meet. You should have been a movie-star.

Of course, the truth was far from being so glamorous. You were singing Joni Mitchell's 'Blue' on the karaoke. I dropped my pint the moment it was handed to me across the bar; and ruined the ending. You could have been angry – quick to give me a piece of your mind; but you didn't. Instead you laughed into the microphone, whilst the screens behind you all turned blue. And that sound, echoing through the place…

I was stolen from where I watched in the crowd.
The tornado had arrived.

I remember apologising to you afterwards. Offering to make it up to you, somehow. And before long, we were making plans to have coffee, drinks, gallery visits and bargain-hunting in backstreet vinyl shops.

You introduced me to Picasso. You showed me how the faces fit together in their lurid-at-first-glance colours, and jigsaw-piece features. You taught me about the blues. You took me home to listen to all of your favourites.

B.B., Elvis, Buddy, and Ray.

Janis, Jimi, Etta and Ella.

Aretha, Billie, Willie and Fats.

And we smoked and talked, and I learned to love your music. I learned so much about you from what was important to you. What made you feel.

We shared our first kiss – do you remember? Under half-hearted protest, you made me watch a VHS of *Lady Sings The Blues*, and by the time the screen turned off, emitting nothing but blue static; our lips somehow found each other. We were bathed in blue light.

The house had finally landed.

And from there, it all happened so quickly. It's been years, but it feels like I've barely had time to blink.

Trips to the beach, feeling the pebbles between our toes. Holding hands, and walking by the ocean.

Picnics in the park, laying out our blankets, and watching clouds float by in a vast, open sky.

Your favourite velveteen sweater, and all the places we took it. All the sights it had seen.

112

That day you lost a shoe on the carousel, and nobody could find it.

The icing roses on our cake, that stained our lips and mouths and tongues.

The way the sunlight warmed your eyes, and lit them up.

I remember who I was before I met you; but only in shades of grey.

But every moment after has been so vivid, and so full of colour; I knew I wasn't dreaming. Only true artists dream like this. And I, love, have never been an artist.

That was all you.

So here we are.

I remember everything about you, everything about us, that brought us to this very spot.

And I want so badly, to know for sure, that I have brought colour to your life, as you have mine.

But I guess we'll never know.

This is my last memory of you, my love.

Standing vigil at your beside, begging those brilliant blue eyes of yours to blink once more.

How do we measure the worth of our lives?

In how we change? How we age? How we are eaten away at all of our hard edges?

Our skin, our voices, our health, our hairlines. Everything eventually dissolves to nothing.

We measure the value of life in time.

But I measure time in shades of blue.

Blue songs are like tattoos...
Picasso's Blue period.
Blue lips.

113

Blue noses.
Kansas City Blues.
B.B., Elvis, Buddy, and Ray.
Janis, Jimi, Etta and Ella.
Aretha, Billie, Willie and Fats.
Blue cigar smoke.
Lady sings the Blues.
Blue screens.
Blue oceans.
Blue skies.
Your favourite blue sweater.
My blue jeans with the faded knees.
Blue fairground horses.
Blue fondant roses.
Blue kisses.
Blue tongues.
Blue veins.
Blue eyes.

Our blues.

I don't know what to do, my love.

Don't know how or even if I'll cope. I don't know what the future holds, but I know this.

I will never find another you.

You have changed me, blowing into my life on a fickle wind, and dropping me over the rainbow.

No matter who, or how I love from now on; I will never shake this final memory.

Your skin, with a tinge of yellow.

Your face, gaunt, but as beautiful as ever.

And your lips. As grey as childhood memories, but just this side of blue.

About the author

Christopher Bowles is an award-winning playwright and performance poet on the Northern spoken word scene. Since founding *Magpie Man Theatre* in 2015, he has written and directed three works, including a solo show adapted from his debut flash-fiction collection *Spectrum* (Chapeltown).

He has previously appeared in four Bridge House anthologies, (*Snowflakes, Baubles, Glit-er-ary,* and *Crackers*), and his fable *The Virtuous Farmer* was included in the Waterloo Festival's 2018 collection.

The Undermen

Louise Rimmer

Mother was in denial, but Father knew that I knew. At dinner, he would gauge my reaction to his comments about the *undermen*, and his story of the boy who had never seen the sun.

"She knows, Alice. She's outsmarted us again," Father laughed, dipping his head towards my mother with an impressed smirk. He reclined contentedly in his seat as he goaded my curious mind.

"Ruben. Enough!" Mother spliced the conversation with a wide eyed, clipped whisper. I wondered why she whispered, as she was fully aware that I could hear her. Father would follow her orders but offer me a wink. *To be continued*, it signalled.

He called me Chi. It means life force, he tells me. I'm practically the size of an adult, but he still cups my face in his masculine-but-soft computer scientist's hands and squeezes me with adoration and frustration. He tells me I have a fire in me that he cannot find. I am his beautiful mutant.

Sometimes he ruminates on my existence, appearing to speak to me but actually talking to himself.

"Just look at you. You know, I used to think that I could create an algorithm for everything and anything. And then you were born, and I saw that there was something else in us that is harder to quantify. But I *will* quantify it. One day I will."

Father works at Infinity Mutations. Their tagline: Choose your Evolution. I'm in their hospital wing today to get some basic adaptations done. I'm having the bridge of my nose widened and my eye colour changed. They're a

116

glittering emerald at the moment, but today they will become deep brown with flecks of magenta.

It's not all cosmetic. I'm also having some rewiring done. I lost a relay race at school last week and Father says my reaction times aren't perfect, so the surgeon will rearrange the appropriate neurons to maximise my reflexive potential.

It's a very simple set of procedures, but I'll be on the ward overnight. This presents a chance to talk to Father without Mother's nervous interruptions.

I already know a little about what Father does. I know that he is a celebrity among scientific circles. I know that he invented and pioneered most of the algorithms at Infinity Mutations. I know that I was born mutated, programmed to reach my human potential. Aside from the standard eradications of disease and disability, Father also enhanced a variety of characteristics during my time in utero. He maximised my physical strength, logical reasoning, critical thinking and empathy.

I also know that there is something I don't know. The *undermen*.

We are alone in the recovery suite. I go easy at first, asking questions about how the business started. Father describes his first invention. A thin, bullet-resistant membrane that can be implanted into human skin.

"People just wouldn't stop shooting each other. Wow, they loved their guns." He shakes his head with a smile of derision and nostalgia for a world I cannot picture. "What was I to do – campaign for a change in gun control laws? Yeah, right."

He scoffs at the notion of himself on a picket line trying to effect social change. I nod in solemn agreement. Peacefully protesting against governments was indeed a fruitless and laughable exercise.

117

"So, I invented a *real* solution. I let the idiots carry on shooting and just made myself bulletproof. And it caught on."

I interrogate. He gives me more.

"OK, Chi. If you're old enough to formulate the question, you're old enough to deal with the answer. The *undermen*. They live underground."

"Where underground?"

"Everywhere, Chi."

I look to the floor. My imagination summons images so vivid they cause the earth to contort underneath my feet. I grab the smooth, steel bedframe. It numbs my hand pleasantly.

"What's it like down there? "

"It will be hard for you to imagine. It's a different existence, my Chi. Let's start with death. You and I know that our deaths will be peaceful. We will be old, probably about one hundred and fifty. Dying will be a *choice*. Our bodies and minds will have weakened, we will be using up valuable resources, and we will have achieved our goals and watched our children grow. It will be time."

I nod, widening my shining new brown-pink eyes.

"And until I create the programming to conquer death, this is the best situation we have."

"I know, Father."

"Down there, death chooses them. It comes suddenly. Unexpectedly."

I stare blankly, unable to process this horrific concept.

"Are there no doctors?"

"They have doctors, but they are primitive. They can't save everyone. And the people aren't like us. They suffer with incurable illnesses. Medieval illnesses. Cancer. Heart disease."

"*Cancer*? But those illnesses are extinct. They said at school. Were they *lying*?"

118

He sits back for a moment to let me figure out this answer for myself.

The sunset is framed neatly by the wide hospital window. Deep red streaks of evening light billow slowly from the horizon, like the silent aftermath of some missile strike or forest fire.

"Can't we help them?"

"Maybe we could, but if we allowed them into our society, they would drag us down. We would *devolve*. Society has to move at the rate of the slowest, Chi. Evolution is survival of the fittest. You know that."

He leans in, his golden eyes burning.

"We are gods; we are transformed. Look at us. We're almost perfect. But to get here, we had to leave some people behind. We didn't bring the apes along when we evolved into humans, did we? And they're doing fine." He raises his palms to the sky, shrugging, as if he has no real control. "It's progression. And you're lucky to be on the right side. Ahead of the curve."

"But why do we deserve to evolve when the other humans don't?"

"'We've earned our places here."

"How do you know?"

"Because I was the boy who never saw the sun."

About the author

Louise is an emerging writer from Merseyside. She enjoys writing about dystopian futures, philosophy and the quirks of the human condition. Her short stories have been published on Inktears.com and in the HG Wells Competition Anthology. She spends most of her free time cleaning up after her two children and her cat. She loves dark humour, loud guitars, bright nail varnish and rough seas. Tweet @Rimmertime

The Word Has It

Hannah Retallick

Transforming.

That's it. I am transforming.

Quite a long word. It carries so much hope. A big weight for any word.

The foundation is on, my face prepared. Now then, should it be eyeshadow before mascara? Maybe I won't do any eyeshadow, just in case. 1975 it was, the risk that blighted my wedding photos.

The eye palette returns to the pink Estee Lauder makeup bag. My granddaughter would tell me to ditch mascara too, because it's gross. Apparently, it's not right to spit in a block anymore – germs, germs, germs. She tried to get me to buy a tube once, but even they expire. Right, a little concealer, a hint of blush, and a dab of old rosy lipstick.

My hair is as grey as donkeys, and I'm never changing that, not even for him. I shouldn't wipe away the years, the highs, the lows, the boring days that now seem sparkly. Even transforming has its limits: the grey hair stays, the mint tea stays, and podgy pug Mervin stays. Goodness, that sounds slightly shallow – I should have said my good heart, steely core, and fiery passion for justice. Since David died, these have remained and increased; I mean the good heart, steely core, and fiery passion for justice. Although, having said that, the mint tea consumption is getting out of hand and I wouldn't like to discuss Mervin's rotundity...

I know I'm moving a little off topic now, as usual, but how much thought can really be put into lip lining? Charles will see the change in me, couldn't fail to, and that's what he'll say when he opens the door: What a transformation! He will look down, blushing slightly, nose lost in the red carnations he brought because he's a listener and he knows they're my favourite. David listened too, especially when I became so quiet that he could almost hear the clock's ticking and the vehement thoughts whirring in my head. I don't remember David buying me flowers though, and I don't know for sure that Charles will – it's just the way he nodded when I said. I wonder if I'm boring to like such a basic bloom, but I can't help it, and I'd rather be happy with carnations than any other flower. Charles reassured me on that count, saying that they were a joyful choice, and all the lovelier for being inexpensive and lasting for a good long while.

This afternoon, he arrives a little before our agreed time of two-thirty and that's fine with me because I've been standing in the hallway for ten minutes already. It seems I've been thrown back a few decades, with a quivering stomach and the other strange symptoms of first love, even though we three were friends for years. I'm certain David would have approved of all this, just as I'm certain he's looking down and smiling, relishing our happiness and waiting to see where these developments might lead. Charles looks down, blushing slightly, nose lost in the red carnations he brought because he knows they're my favourite, and I lean forward to wrap my arms around his shaking shoulders. I'm glad I ditched the purple eyeshadow – it wouldn't have scared Charles, just as it didn't scare David, although that says more about them as men than it does about the eyeshadow. You look beautiful, he says, and he passes me the flowers, wrapped in clear plastic with the price still attached and clearly visible to me; we both know their cost and their worth. There are white ones mixed in with them, which is perfect because those are the ones he prefers, as he told me the other day; I like a man who has a favourite carnation. Poised on the bristly brown doormat, cheeks burning with new youth, I've become a basic bloom; happy, inexpensive, I've lasted a good long while, and intend to last a good while longer: transforming and transformed.

About the author

Hannah Retallick is a twenty-six-year-old from Anglesey, North Wales. She was home educated and then studied with the Open University, graduating with a First-class honours degree, BA in Humanities with Creative Writing and Music, before passing her Creative Writing MA with a Distinction. She was shortlisted in the Writing Awards at the Scottish Mental Health Arts Festival 2019, the Cambridge Short Story Prize, the Henshaw Short Story Competition June 2019, and the Bedford International Writing Competition 2019.

https://ihaveanideablog.wordpress.com/

They Lied to Me

Madeleine McDonald

They lied to me, Mum and Charlie. I can't forgive them that. I'll never forgive them.

Alistair Kaplan, that's my name. Can't get more English than that, can you? I was married in our parish church and that wouldn't have been allowed, if I wasn't English. Wendy's family weren't too keen. They're Welsh. Funny lot, the Welsh. Wendy's parents objected because the family was Chapel not Church. Whereas me, I thought St Cuthbert's perfect for a wedding. Right in the heart of the village, and dating back to fourteen hundred and something. It stood there when we won at Agincourt. I'm not religious but there's something about a church spire that makes a village look right. We took some lovely photos that day.

The vicar didn't mind that Wendy was Chapel. I waved my Sunday School attendance certificates under his nose and made a donation to the restoration fund. I forget which bit of the church was falling down that year. Our wedding was 40 years ago, and details elude me.

But I remember Sunday School. Sunday School was boring but Charlie insisted, and when Charlie said something, we didn't argue. "Your Dad said it was important," he told me. "So you and your sister are going."

That wasn't the lie. It was Dad who lied. Charlie just carried on the family tradition.

Mum married Charlie after Dad died. I'd like to remember my Dad but I've only got fragments of memory, like peeking through the banisters and seeing a tall man bring a red bicycle into the hallway, and bubbling over with excitement 'cause the bicycle was my Christmas present.

It was Charlie who told me about his workmate Joe, and the other brickies on the team. When I was about eight years old I got a big blister on my finger. Charlie taught me to pop the blister open and pee on it. "This is tricks of the trade, Al. Your dad and me did this regular." I yelped when the pee stung me, but I swaggered back to the house feeling all grown up.

Salt of the earth was Charlie. We put flowers on his grave every year. Mum, me and Wendy, my sister Sarah and her husband. That's how I found out.

When I rang Mum and suggested a date for our trip to the cemetery, she said she couldn't make it because she was going to Turkey. Well, I thought she was off on a Saga holiday, a bit of sun for the oldies. "No," she told me, "I may be away some time."

Turned out she meant to go exploring deep into the mountains of Eastern Turkey, where Dad's family came from. What? My grandparents came here in 1926, almost a hundred years ago. No-one will remember them.

So I put my foot down. Dad's dead, Charlie's dead, I'm the head of the family now.

"Mum," I said. "You can't go. It's not safe. What if you get mugged? What if you need a doctor?" Mum had a hip replacement last year, and she takes pills for blood pressure.

I heard obstinacy in her voice. "I promised Yussuf."

Yussuf? Was Mum losing her marbles? "Mum, Dad's name was Joseph."

"He was Yussuf when I married him."

That was news to me. Everyone called him Joe. "Dad was born here," I reminded her. "He was English, not Turkish. His birth certificate says Joseph."

I was taken aback by the bitterness in her answer. "He was born here, but he was always an outsider. He didn't

124

speak any different, he didn't look much different, but people knew his family was foreign."

Can't say I'm surprised when I think about it. Though, what with the state she was in, I couldn't say that to Mum. I guess it is tough being a foreigner here, but I'm proud of my country. It's in my bones, in my blood. If people come to this country they ought to make an effort to fit in instead of biting the hand that feeds them. I don't like it when I see all these shops with Polish writing in the window. And don't get me started on the bloody Arabs blowing us up. Charlie would have a fit if he saw what's happening now. There's no respect any more. No jobs for our kids because of foreigners taking over.

The more I argued, the more Mum dug her heels in. "I'm 86," she told me. "I was dealing with practicalities when you were in nappies, my lad. You try getting on and off a bus with two toddlers and a load of shopping."

I did try to put her straight. "Mum," I said. "Have you considered… I mean this is the 21st century, and we have to be broad-minded and all that, and it is their culture, but you do realise, don't you, Mum, that most Turks are Muslims."

That's when she told me my grandparents were Muslim.

She's winding me up! Dad was English. I'm English. I knew his parents were Turkish, but I thought… I thought they were people like us. Normal people.

Mum got cross. "It's a mercy your grandparents aren't alive to hear you deny them," she said. "Of course they were Muslims. It's a Muslim country."

So how come I went to Sunday School? Turns out Dad wanted me and Sarah to fit in, because he never did. No-one ever told me I was part Muslim.

They lied to me. I can't forgive them that.

Turns out my granddad fought at Gallipoli. Our brave

lads signed up in 1914 to defend civilisation and my granddad did the same – on the other side. So what if he was only fifteen at the time? Right now, I wish he had stayed put and never come here. Though I suppose that would have made me well and truly Muslim.

But I'm not. I'm me.

I am not a bloody foreigner!

About the author
Madeleine McDonald lives in Yorkshire, where the cliffs crumble into the sea. She finds inspiration walking on the beach before the world wakes up.

Time Will Tell

Michael Baez

Maxine Trenton majored in Alternate History in every multiverse: In B5 she was dead; in C3 she was famous; in D9 she was married; and in E1 she dared break the law.

The Trans-dimensional bracelet didn't care which wrist Maxine strapped it on. It always made her tremble. Maxine's conscience was placed on hold: time gave her little choice.

"Bubble universes don't exist," Maxine muttered for the hundredth time. Continuum Scholars disagreed. If they were right, going back was meaningless. Maxine crossed her fingers, clinging to hope. Her will steeled, unbreakable as her ammolite earrings. She'd lost her morals and the better half of Earth – being optimistic was all she had left.

"Maxine, dear, supper's ready," Grell's voice snaked through the cracks.

The taste of blueberry smoothies for breakfast, lunch, and dinner lingered on Maxine's throat. Frozen foods repulsed her. The scorching sun branded her.

Maxine mouthed a goodbye. Facing Grell would only give her a reason to stay.

Sunlight pierced through Maxine's window, melting reinforced glass. The shades caught a blaze. A flash followed – the solar flare. Screams echoed in the distance. Sparks burst from Maxine's intergalactic radio. Photographs of birthdays and ex-girlfriends turned to ash. Memories disintegrated.

Dust lingered in the wake of crumbling skyscrapers. Walls dissolved around her.

Maxine could already read the headlines: 'Millions Dead in Seconds'.

Maxine tugged on her bracelet, leaving everything behind.

Every T-officer described *the passing* as a moment – a blink – but Maxine saw more. Ancestors sped past her in rewind. She ached to stop the clock and know them all. To converse about the weather back when it wasn't killing anyone. But she knew better. The Trans-dimensional bracelet wouldn't stop once it had its coordinates. Nothing, not even removing it, could change that. She'd already broken enough laws for a lifetime; she had no intention of breaking the multiverse.

The passing ceased. Maxine's lineage withered with it.

A salty wind hugged her as the year 2065 settled.

Maxine gawked at her hands, unbelieving. The bracelet's silver bead throbbed as time wound on. She stuck out her tongue and saline made her taste buds yearn for more. The chilled waves crashed against the dock, and gusts danced with her brunette locks.

"Business," Maxine shuddered with the breeze. As much as she yearned to sightsee, time was her enemy.

Yachts, cruises, and boats replaced the crowded, fume infested parking lots. Maxine couldn't fathom how the sea had vanished and left a vast desert behind. Seeing it all with her own eyes made the unfeasible possible.

Her mark, The Copernicus, was tucked between a yacht and a dinghy. Maxine slithered behind a bush and tapped her wrist for the time. Six-thirty. Just like the books in D9 and B5.

The blood orange sunset hypnotized Maxine. She ogled the view thankful that she wouldn't spontaneously combust, when out of the corner of her eye she saw the two lovers snuggling beside a warm fire. Heat made Maxine flinch, but the scent of trout enthralled her. It taunted her, burrowed into her nostrils, beckoning. She resisted.

Maxine fled from one bush to another. Dipping her hand into her pocket, she felt the cold grip of the stolen incinerator. Death's chill stiffened her heart. With one eye closed, and what was left of her morals withering away, she aimed. No! Maxine stashed it back in her pocket. To replicate history, she had to follow it to the letter.

"Skinny dipping," Maxine said as she remembered B5's death certificate.

"Awesome idea," the burly man said.

Maxine's hand darted to her mouth and she swallowed a curse. Grell always told her that big mouth would be the end of her. She couldn't wait any longer.

Scrambling past bushes and branches, Maxine reached the lake. She tapped her neck and gills emerged from her mahogany skin. Stealing from the old veterinary museum would finally pay off. Maxine plunged into the water. Warmth enveloped her at the bottom of the lake. Translucent fish swam by like ghosts. Maxine reached out, mesmerized, but they scurried away.

Splash!

The couple intertwined in the murky waters. Their silhouettes caught Maxine's careful eye. Her hand hesitated; her fingers curled into fists, refusing. Withering integrity withheld her hand momentarily. Maxine grappled onto the dame's ankle and jerk – hard!

Within seconds, the woman was under. She kicked and thrashed. Maxine covered her mouth until all that remained was an unsettling stillness. She let go of the body and it surfaced, limp. Maxine followed a close second. Her heart skipped various beats. Murder didn't weigh on her as much as having to face him.

As he held his lover, desperation soaking his eyes, remorse didn't burden Maxine.

"Can I have your autograph?" Maxine blurted out. The

tattoo pen trembled in her hand, wet with ink. There she was, swimming beside the soon-to-be savior of Earth, and it was all thanks to her. Maxine shook her head. "Don't worry about her. She was going to kill you anyway."

About the author
Michael Baez lives in Puerto Rico in a tiny apartment with an even tinier desk. He has a bachelor's degree in theology and a minor in Teaching English as a Second Language. He strives to bring a Puerto Rican flair to the writing community. At the moment, he is pursuing an Ed.D. Michael has published in Revista Trasuntos, Rigorous Magazine, Corpus Litterarum, and The Hound Magazine.

Transforming Communities

Winning entries from the 2020 Waterloo Festival Writing Competition

Foreword by Debz Hobbs-Wyatt

As part of the small team at Bridge House Publishing, I have had the pleasure of being able to read and help select the stories for the Waterloo Festival Writing Competition for the past three years. The theme has always been connected to the idea of transformation: transforming minds, transforming being and this time **transforming communities**. Of course, at the time the theme for this year was announced, we could never have anticipated what 2020 would bring or the impact that would have on all our communities globally.

Covid-19 has clearly had a major impact on what it feels to be part of a community. It has touched all aspects of our lives, including how even this collection is launched and how the 2020 festival is run. The good thing is that at no other time in history have we had so much technology at our fingertips to make that possible. In modern life, we already know about *virtual* communities, some even fall in love that way, and now we have realised the real importance of making our connections through different means. Of course, that is no substitute of the warmth of a real hug – but those days will return when we will once again close the two-metre gap and understand that part of community we are closed off to at the time of putting this collection together. If that has happened, go hug someone right now and appreciate something as simple as that. Perhaps not if you're reading this on a train full of strangers!

Community for me is connection. We connect, we come together, we support, as you will see in the stories in this collection. But connection also has its dark side, as we will also have seen at this strange time in our history, perhaps non-conformity is equally part of community.

You will see community explored in the most diverse of ways in this little book. From a mining community trying to save the planet but at the same time *killing* its workers, children who disappear, segregation according to colour but not as we know it, though disturbingly similar. You will read about a book club for the elderly, about storytelling, about communities who come together at times of adversity… each story unique and exploring the theme in new and interesting ways.

There were stories I loved that I almost chose for the collection but this for me had everything I felt a collection about transforming communities needed. At this current time of *transformed communities* one thing you can always rely on – **writers will write, stories will be read and people will find ways to come together.**

Enjoy and well done to all of those who made this collection possible. Even if you did not make it into the collection this time, we enjoyed reading the stories and there's always next time!

Debz Hobbs-Wyatt
May 2020

Dolly

Mehreen Ahmed

"Not without her," Ana screamed. "I'm not leaving without Dolly."

But the police officer kept pestering. She put Ana's hands in hand-cuff. Ana yelled at the constable. She told Ana that she must leave without her doll. For it was really she who was in trouble, not her doll. Ana realised that police officer didn't understand that Dolly was her security blanket, now and always. Ever since she was five, now fifteen.

"Trouble?" she screamed. You say, I'm in trouble? A parasite? Under the radar until you caught me out?"

"What else would you call yourselves? You, downy mildews of fester? You steal buns from that bakery, there.

"I only steal for hunger."

"Little snitch! I'll get you sorted out."

"Ha! You make me laugh. I have been like this since five. I sold flowers on Harlon Street, an orphan, and a phantom to most. Those who saw my flowers, never saw me; invisible like a camouflaged screech owl on a living bark. Then one day, someone noticed me," she said.

"Who? Who noticed you?" asked the police constable.

"He did. The big man. One evening, it rained. I appeared at his car window with a bunch of yellow chrysanthemums. He rolled down his windows and offered me money. He told me to take the money, and re-sell the wet bunch. Just when the lights changed, I dropped the flowers on his lap, saying that he must take them or else Dolly would get offended and she would punish me. The man drove away."

She looked down at the grooved pavement littered with

torn plastic bags. A bed made out of slippery bags for a slippery life. Her doll lay there, too.

"Is this a way to live? You should be ashamed of your life?" the constable yelled.

"Yeah? You have a better idea? Where were you when they took me? Those big men's playing doll that I had almost become. Where were you when those leeches nearly lay me down in their valley? The dark night's under-bridge."

Another rain began as Ana told her story, how the same car came back the next night, and she, a mere child of ten, ran towards it to sell some more. But this time the driver opened the car door instead of a window. He tried to entice her with bundle loads of money. But she thought of Dolly. She wouldn't go anywhere without Dolly. The girl ran away this night.

The end of her flower-selling days came the next evening. This time she had Dolly with her. That car was on the street. She stood squeezed in between the traffic jam. Two strong hands grabbed her and pulled her inside.

She fretted, twisted and turned. Ana fell asleep. The car sped along; they reached a mansion. The heavy doors opened, a woman appeared. She came to the car and took Ana inside. They entered a pink bedroom. She scoffed at her, "Not another word." Weeks and months passed. She was kept all to herself in this pink bedroom. It was full of dolls. The woman dolled her up too, beautiful dresses, and new make-up. But she missed her street.

Then one day, the man summoned her into the living room, she hadn't seen in many days. But he wasn't alone. He was with others.

"What's your name, little girl?" asked another man.

She replied, shyly, "Ana,"

"Lovely name, Ana. Go pack a small bag, I want to take you out."

A cold shiver ran through her. She was going out with this strange man. Maybe, this could open up an escape route. In her room, she packed a pink suitcase and picked up Dolly. She came back into the living room. The man took her hand and walked her out of the palace. Ana never saw this palace again, the woman, or the first man. They climbed into another car that the new man drove. In the car, he looked at her and slid his hand under Ana's skirt. Ana felt odd. She tried to move away from him. By now he had started his car, and the car sped down a highway.

"Where are you taking me?" Ana asked.

"You'll see. Don't be afraid."

Ana began to cry. She screamed so much that the man had to stop his car. He took Ana by her shoulders, and shook them.

"Stop this. Stop this at once. Or else I'll kill you."

Ana cowed before his rage. He glowered at her and restarted his car. She looked at her doll and pressed her close to her chest. Her nails dug deep into the doll's cascading hair. She thought of her flowers, the delicate white, yellow, pink chrysanthemum petals. How they bloomed before her and perished. Her freedom on the street, her kind boss, the owner of the flower shop. Some days, she got paid, some days, she didn't. Some days she ate, some days she didn't. It all depended on the sale. But this? Anything was better than this. She fought her miserable thoughts. This new place, she didn't know. Where was she going to go? The driver stopped the car, yet again. He got out, locking her inside. Ana's restive mind thought of a way out. She held her Dolly tight and said.

136

"Dear Dolly, I will take you out of here. I won't let that bastard touch you."

The doll looked at her and blinked. Something clicked. There was a sound of the locks popping straight up. The car doors flung open. Bright lights in her eyes, Dolly smiled. Ana was free. She jumped out of the car. She fled. She fled with Dolly and never looked back. The man had gone to buy coffee, she imagined. She pictured him back into the car, looking frantically for Ana. But all he found was her pink suitcase, perched neatly against the seat's leather-back.

About the author

Mehreen Ahmed is an award-winning, internationally published and critically acclaimed author. She has written novels, novella, short stories, creative nonfiction, flash fiction, academic, prose poetry, memoirs, essays and journalistic write-ups. Her works have been podcast, anthologised and translated in German, Greek and Bengali. She has two master's degrees and a bachelor's (Hon) in English Literature and Linguistics from the University of Queensland and Dhaka University. She was born and raised in Bangladesh. At the moment, she lives in Australia.

The Price of Firewood

Gail Aldwin

Dust covered her hands as Beatrice picked another twig from the ground. That morning she'd washed in water from the borehole and there had been a lustre to her skin. But now she look and felt more like a crinkled passion fruit. Tssk. If Mama was there and could read her mind, she'd scold Beatrice for being vain. Easing free another bit of wood half buried in earth, Beatrice was reminded of the tomato plant that showed promise when the shoot burst through the soil only to flop and die. Mama said the garden was rubbish. How can we be expected to grow vegetables amongst the rocks and stones on this camp? Beatrice sighed and tugged at another stubborn twig. It came out knotted and bent like Gramma's fingers. Those hands had once tied fancy braids in Beatrice's hair. Back when she went to school and lessons were taught in her own language. She remembered how Gramma had fastened buttons at the back of her tunic. Beatrice straightened, dropped the twig to join the others at the bottom of her sack. For a moment, she felt the weight of her school uniform and the skirt brushing her calves. But she scrubbed the memory just as she had to forget about Gramma. It did no good to think about whether Gramma was still in the village. Mama said soldiers wouldn't waste a bullet on her and Beatrice hoped she was right.

Morning breath was fresh. Breezes tamed the early sun which was not too bright or hot. Picking firewood was Beatrice's first job of the day. The long branches were already gone – there must have been others at work earlier than she. But Beatrice didn't like collecting in half light. That was when danger lurked and boys goaded. She didn't want to come face-to-face with them again. Instead, she found what firewood she could along the roadside, across the scrub. The bits and pieces were not enough even for a small fire. She pressed on, making more effort she bent and stretched. One girl was returning, a neat bundle balanced on her head but Beatrice's sack was not half full. There would be a quarrel at home if she didn't bring more.

Mama sucked breath when she saw the pickings. More was needed to cook beans and asida. Now we are eight, Mama reminded. Gerald was the latest. Mama had wiped the stripes of tear trails from his face and brought him home from the food distribution point. Aunty had walked him to safety and left him there. He brought no news from our village. He had no words to tell. His voice will come, Mama said. Yes, Gerald was the latest. Another child to feed but Mama can stretch the flour and beans a little further.

After school, Mama sent Beatrice to pick firewood. Oh no, please no! But it was her job as the eldest girl. It was for her to do. Danger loitered in long shadows: locals who mocked the refugee girls. And things happened that she should never tell. So the sticks she got and the price she paid and the tears that came. But she couldn't tell, not even to Mama… the shame was too much. And as long as she hoped and she prayed, her belly would not ripen. It would not be Beatrice who brought another mouth to feed into the home.

About the author

Gail Aldwin is a novelist, poet and scriptwriter. Her debut novel *The String Games* was a finalist in The People's Book Prize and the DLF Writing Prize 2020. Her first children's picture book *Pandemonium* was published in 2020. Gail regularly appears at literary and fringe festivals. Prior to Covid-19, Gail volunteered at Bidibidi in Uganda, the second largest refugee settlement in the world. Her home overlooks water meadows in Dorset.

Chroma

Christopher Bowles

CHROMA:

The first recorded incident occurred in the sixteenth century. Physicians wrote the following on the birth of Veronica Whyte:

> *The babe was stillborn to Poppy and Forrest Whyte, to rampant rumour and accusations of witchcraft; as the girl emerged into the world, not with the pure white skin expected of every newborn, but instead dyed a brilliant shade of cornflower blue.*

The next occasion wasn't officially recorded until nearly a hundred years later, a bright-green boy born to Violet and Grayham Wan; named Tanner. (Although historians widely agree that there were likely several other occurrences in the meantime; either discreetly terminated or hidden from the annals of history.) This coincided with numerous notable outbreaks of contagious disease; and the census of the time are deemed largely unreliable due to the wildly fluctuating death rates.

Over the next century, numerous other incidents emerged; a set of twins in China, and three separate childbirths in insular environments – indigenous tribes in Africa and the Amazon. The Xi twins were considered omens of bad luck, and as a result remained unnamed. They were recorded as deceased only two years later; classified as 'deaths of indeterminate cause' and without further inquest. The three tribal offspring were all revered in their communities and raised in sacred positions of the community, but due to the isolated nature of their upbringings, details remained sparse.

Whilst initially assumed to be a familial genetic mutation; not dissimilar to albinism or vitiligo, Geneticists were unable to determine the likelihood of such births, nor isolate the gene that caused the effect. Interestingly, most recorded cases involved individuals living well into adulthood; and several papers were researched into whether earlier cases of infant-death were due to societal pressure or simply a lack of medical aptitude.

Heading into the twentieth century, these incidents of what was eventually coined Chromaticism (sic) became commonplace enough to spark off widespread societal micro-aggressions, and segregational hate-crimes. Recorded incidents of designated public drinking-fountains and seating areas on public transport; for fear of contagion, although this was widely discredited by both the W.H.O. and the C.D.C.

Worldwide protests emerged, and in conservative areas of the United States, a national emergency was declared following wide-scale riots and violent disturbances. National newspapers began regularly featuring Chromatic citizens as scapegoats for local crimes; and were deemed largely responsible for a great period of civil unrest. The Herald published a story where three Chromatic citizens were burned alive at the stake.

There grew an increased interest in determining the origin of the condition; many directors and cinematic houses seized the opportunity to determine it must be a side-effect of alien contact; or divine intervention. Several exploitative movies were spawned in quick succession, including the controversial Oscar-winning *Attack of the Coloured People* (dir. Roan Piebald 1997).

It became commonplace for television serials to include a token Chromatic character; although mostly stereotypical villainous tropes. Several high-profile academic essays were released, detailing the problematic treatment of Chromatic characters in cinematic media. This fuelled a social movement; sparking the controversial introduction of skin dyes into the market; where typical citizens were able to purchase home-kits in order to temporarily stain themselves in solidarity.

National governments began to work on developing segregated safe-zones for 'sufferers' to live in relative peace; but this was widely condemned by the pro-Chroma genetic activist Rosalind Fields. Her later assassination by an Alt-right terrorist cell was at the forefront of media obsession for months.

After several incidents of workplace discrimination; citing unfair dismissal of Chromatic employees; there was an increased number of high-profile cases. This eventually lead to a rewording of the Human Rights Act; re-transcribing the legislation to include more chromatically-friendly language. One notable amendment was the removal of all usages of the derogatory term "Chromatic sufferers".

The first official act of anti-Chromatic terrorism is widely regarded to be the Rainbow massacre in 2008. Teenager Russell "Rusty" Carthage used semi-automatic weapons to assault the Orlando nightclub. Forty-nine combined fatalities and wounded were recorded at the time. Carthage was shot dead on the scene, but investigation into his personal life revealed an online blog where he would regularly post homophobic and chromaphobic abuse; citing his intended attack as:

A cleanse on the human stain

In response to both the public statement made by Pope Lewis in May of 2021 regarding the lack of Chromaticism in holy scriptures (and therefore cementing the position of the church as anti-Chroma) and the eventual election of right-wing Prime Minister Priyanka Garstang in 2022; several pockets of Chromatic radicals emerged; culminating in the failed suicide-bombing at the Vatican in August of the same year, and the later event at Parliament on November 5th. Twenty-four MPs who had voted against Chromatic rights were killed at the scene.

In her second year of office, Garstang controversially resigned following the birth of her granddaughter; who was diagnosed with the condition. The much-publicised divorce of President Duggan; after his wife gave birth to an orange son fuelled months of satirical cartoons and widespread ridicule.

2036 saw the election of the first Chromatic MP; Aurelia Matheson made the following comments following her successful bid on behalf of the Green Party:

I am proud to represent one of the most forward-thinking constituencies in the UK. The people of Bristol West support me one-hundred percent in bringing the plight and views of Chromatic citizens to the forefront of parliament; and I will ensure that our voice is heard.

In December of the following year, there was uproar when the first Chromatic Royal baby was announced. The monarchy refused to comment on the matter and asked the public to respect their privacy; although this was deemed hypocritical and widely criticised in a non-partisan move by the BBC and several global news outlets.

The first recorded incident of a white birth occurred in the early twenty-third century. Elaine Bianco shared the following statement:

My little Halley is fit, healthy and beautiful. She's perfect and that's all that matters.

About the author

Christopher Bowles is an award-winning playwright and National Slam Champion of performance poetry. He founded Magpie Man Theatre in 2015; and recently published his first collection of flash fiction, Spectrum. He is a big fan of both coffee and chocolate, and accepts all donations gladly.

Pulling Together

Maxine Churchman

Ray's shoulders slumped. "I don't think I can do this again, Bet. Three times in five years, it's too much to bear."

Betty looked at the silver flecks in her husband's dark hair; had there been so much grey a few days ago? The strain was getting to her too, but they needed to stay strong. She patted his arm. "We said that last time love, but we got through."

"But look at it. It's far worse than last time. Where do we even start?"

Filth coated everything, and it wasn't just mud; the sewers had been washed out with the flood water. The stench was awful. Last time – two years ago almost to the day – it had taken four weeks to get the pub open again. They'd worked round the clock to refurbish all the downstairs rooms. The new wallpaper, carpets and large pieces of furniture would have to be replaced again.

She made her way behind the bar, her wellies squelching on the sodden carpet, and poured two large whiskeys. "Here, we need this," she said handing one to her husband, "at least the water didn't reach the optics and glasses."

The storm warning had given them enough time to move smaller items upstairs, but all the stock in the cellar would be contaminated.

Ray squeezed her hand. "It's such a shame. The last eight or nine months have been so good."

That was down to Sheila; their bar manager. She believed passionately in bringing people together, and had introduced all sorts of events to bring in the locals.

One of her most popular ideas was in response to the

145

County Council closing their village library. Its closure had been a blow to the community, but Sheila saw opportunities where others saw problems. Bringing the library into the pub seemed like a crazy idea, but she was tenacious and persuasive. She persuaded the council to give them a selection of books and some of the smaller library shelves. The books lined two walls of the lounge bar and were available for anyone to read in the pub, or borrow to take home. Books were often donated by the locals too, so the collection had grown and changed. People, who didn't normally frequent the pub, started coming in on Library afternoons; sometimes just to have a chat or to make friends.

Library afternoons took place every day, after school, and were very popular with parents and their children. The pub made good sales of coffee, soft drinks, crisps and cakes. Sometimes, volunteers read stories and sang nursery rhymes with the little ones. For two hours each afternoon, the pub was a lively hub of the community; something that had been missing from the village before Sheila. She was amazing.

"No more Karaoke, quizzes, folk evenings." Ray's voice was full of regret. Suddenly he lifted his head and smiled. "Where will Bill tell his awful jokes now?"

Betty laughed. It felt good to laugh, but the sadness was still evident in Ray's eyes. She leant in and kissed him tenderly on his cheek. It felt cold against her warm lips.

"Are we disturbing something?" Sheila called, in her loud cheery voice as she pushed the door open. She was wearing overalls and wellies. Her bouncy auburn hair was hidden under a colourful scarf. "I've rallied the troops; we should have this mess cleared in no time."

A dozen people poured in behind her, also dressed for dirty work.

146

"Phew, what a whiff!" Bill said. "You could have changed your socks today, Ray." His big beer belly wobbled as he laughed at his own joke.

Everyone laughed and Betty felt tears prick her eyes. Most of these folks would have their own problems to resolve after the flood. She was touched they were giving up their time to help.

How could they let down such a great community, just because they'd suffered another setback? "Well, Ray?" she asked.

His eyes shone with unshed tears and his lower lip quivered. He bobbed his head and turned away. Only Betty saw the tear slide down his cheek.

"We can't thank you enough," she said to their friends. "Let's get stuck in shall we?"

About the author
Maxine Churchman is a mother and grandmother from Essex UK. Her hobbies include reading, hiking, yoga and, more recently, writing. So far she has concentrated on short stories, but hopes to make progress on a novel in 2020. She has had work published by CaféLit, Black Hare Press, Stormy Island Publishing and Clarendon House Publishing.

http://cccmaxine.blogspot.com

Utopian Trend

Jeanne Davies

Melanie zigzagged down winding lanes, sunshine darting through beech trees onto her dusty window screen. A year had passed since she'd visited Sussex. She reminisced as she approached Burpham, a tiny village saddled to the back of the south downs, before veering off down the quiet lane where she was born. Claypit Lane had been developed, but Perrymead Cottage hadn't changed. Dismissing cascades of tears, she marvelled at Dahlias, and lanky Foxgloves, all testimony to her mother's gardening skills. Nearby Grove Farmhouse had been demolished and replaced by a huge grey building without windows, the adjoining horse-field a vast car park for supermarket lorries.

The heart-wrenching sound of cows as calves were taken still haunted her dreams. Melanie would gaze at fluffy white lambs bouncing in fields, innocently asking her mother why farmers couldn't buy their meat at Sainsbury's like they did. She became vegetarian at twelve, but soon realised this still condoned cows being forcefully impregnated for milk products, so she became vegan at sixteen. Over the years she discovered that being free-range wouldn't save a hen's life; as she aged, and her productivity decreased, her poor worn out body would be used in cheap chicken products like pies and pasties. One-day-old male chicks were destroyed because they couldn't lay eggs. After investigating the dairy and meat producing industries, Melanie created Animal Utopia, with their slogan being "Freedom for anything with a face".

Realising the time, she sped off in the direction of the crematorium hoping to see her mother before the service commenced. Visiting her parents over the past ten years had been sporadic since becoming head of Animal Utopia. She toured many countries giving lectures on how communities and their environments could be changed by veganism. After thirty years of campaigning, forsaking marriage and the chance of a family, she finally saw the fruits of her labours when the government started to pay farmers to produce more arable crops. The landscape in the countryside became transformed with the absence of chicken-coops, pigsties and cattle grazing in the fields.

Arriving late at the crematorium, her brother shot her an angry look as mourners exited the building. He'd always been there for their parents whilst Melanie pursued her career, with his wife Christine supplying them with grandchildren.

"Sorry, Jacob, I didn't mean to miss the service."

Her brother looked straight through her.

"Can I see her before the actual cremation?"

"Yeah, sure, if it makes you feel better about yourself," he said as he walked away.

Melanie swallowed the tears threatening to engulf her again and walked into the chapel.

"I'm Mrs Weatherby's daughter, I'd like to see her please."

"I'll check if that's possible," the black-suited woman replied.

Melanie waited nervously. She'd seen her father in the hospital morgue after his fatal heart attack and he'd looked just like he'd done that morning when he left the cottage. The woman eventually returned stating that, because Mrs Weatherby had donated her organs to medical research, her body was on its way to the local centre where the cremation process would be finalised. Melanie's eyes filled with tears; she hadn't even been able to say a final goodbye.

Bewildered and lost, Melanie wandered aimlessly

towards the small crowd entering the adjacent venue for the wake. Her brother glanced up indignantly and his wife immediately ushered their children inside. At that moment a black ambulance drove past at high speed. Something about it disturbed her; the driver was the woman in the chapel. She made a snap decision to follow it.

Melanie struggled to keep up with the vehicle in front, especially when they encountered the winding country lanes she'd driven down earlier. The black ambulance overtook a tractor and sped off ahead, but she could just see its indicator in the distance heading down Claypit Lane. She followed but decided to park in Perrymeads's driveway and walk. She watched from a distance as the ambulance reversed into a loading bay outside the grey building. A large door was electronically raised, and the black-suited woman supervised the removal of what could only be a body from the boot. After the door closed, she drove off at speed, causing Melanie to duck down behind a bush.

As Melanie approached the loading doors, she read some of the signs, many of which were health and safety related, some stipulating that unauthorised persons would not be permitted to enter the building for hygiene reasons. After pressing buttons on the intercom, a woman's voice said, "Welcome to Grove food processing plant, how can I help you?"

"I'd like to see the manager urgently please!"

"It's an honour to meet you Miss Weatherby! I'm Keith Farlow, proprietor." He was a tall, thin man, she recognised from some of her conferences. "I'm such a huge fan of your organisation and encourage many of my staff to attend your lectures."

"I'm confused," Melanie answered. "This place seems very under cover, exactly what type of food do you process here?"

"It's a new blend of food with a 95% meat content. I can see your disappointment, but please hear me out. I can assure you there is no threat to animal welfare," he said, gesturing for her to sit down. "Not all medical research donors are viable for various reasons, including age. The human brain and organs contain high levels of nutrients and, because there is still a high demand for meat, we create a product which is entirely eco-friendly, cost effective, and eliminates factory farming and cruelty to animals… until meat-eating is finally outlawed."

Melanie was speechless.

"We would be so honoured if you could endorse our products as cruelty free," he added.

Trembling inside, she rose to her feet and walked towards the door.

"Although I believe my dear mother has just been delivered here, I will agree to endorse your product," she sighed. "But I want you to put a slogan beneath its name."

"What should it to say?"

"A cow's revenge."

About the author

Jeanne Davies has always enjoyed making up stories visiting other people's worlds and feelings, and began to submit to competitions a few years back. Seeing them in print is a huge encouragement and motivation. She's been fortunate enough to have short stories, flash fiction and poetry included in various anthologies and magazines, and her single author anthology *Drawn by the Sea* has recently been published by Bridge House.

A Small Clay Vase

Jo Dearden

Jan is listening to the afternoon play on the radio as she works her way through a pile of ironing in her small but spotlessly clean kitchen. This is one of her favourite times in the day when she can immerse herself in another world. It is stiflingly hot. She has the kitchen window open and can hear the incessant hum of the traffic on the road below their flat. Her husband Stuart is out doing a few errands. He still hasn't got used to not working since he retired from his builder's job a few months ago.

He has too much time to think, Jan thought sadly. He has always felt bitter that we were unable to have children, a blight that has cast a dark shadow over our lives. We were so happy once. But at least we now have Elbaz to look after. Elbaz – such a scrap of a thing when he arrived. He looked half-starved in dirty ragged clothes and shoes that were too big for him. He didn't speak for the first few days but stared at us with his large dark brown eyes as if we were aliens. I suppose Syria is very different to England and goodness knows what he had suffered with the terrible war.

Her reverie is suddenly broken by the sound of the front door opening.

"Hello love," Stuart called as he came into the flat carrying a heavy shopping bag. Jan started to put away her ironing board.

"Shall I make us a cup of tea," she said as Stuart heaved his heavy frame onto one of the kitchen chairs.

"That'd be grand," he said. "Is Elbaz not back yet?"

"No, I think he said he had to stay for something after school today."

She put the kettle on. "Did you manage to get everything?"

152

Stuart looked up from the newspaper he'd bought. "Yeah, I think so." Jan began to unpack the shopping bag.

The doorbell rang. It was Martha, their new neighbour. "Hi there," she said. She was wearing a white vest top with skinny blue jeans and jewelled flip flops. Her blonde hair scooped up in a tortoiseshell clip. Gold bangles on her suntanned arms jangled as she spoke. "You know, me and Dave would like to, well you know, make this place look a bit nicer," she said.

"Well yes, we'd heard about your plans, but we can't afford it. I'm sorry. It's a nice idea but no one in these flats is very well off," said Jan.

"I'm only thinking of a few plants and may be some nice outside furniture. Oh, and we could do with replacing the paving as well. It would really make the community area look so much nicer. Something we'd all use, especially like now in hot weather," Martha explained.

"Not sure where you'll get the money from," Jan said half closing the door.

"Anyway, I just came to tell you that we want to get everyone together to have a meeting about it. We can probably all squeeze into our living room as ours is one of the larger flats. Shall we say next Saturday at 6 o" clock?"

Jan hesitated. "Oh good. See you then. Must go. Bye," Martha called as she walked away.

"Well the cheek of the woman," Jan said as she came back into the kitchen.

"What did she want?"

"She wants us to go to a meeting about making the communal space nicer."

"Well, she can stuff her fancy ideas. Who does she think she is anyway," Stuart said as he tossed the paper onto the kitchen table and slammed the door as he went outside.

Jan felt hot tears prick behind her eyes. It was as if it

was her fault. She knew she found Martha difficult to stand up to. She was well meaning but had managed to annoy everyone since moving in a few weeks ago. They had a lot on their plate now with having to care for Elbaz. When the leaflet had come through the door asking if anyone would be prepared to take in a refugee, it had seemed a good idea. "When have we ever done anything to help anyone?" Jan had said to Stuart. He hadn't taken much persuading. Their childless lives had seemed even emptier than before, since he had stopped working.

Jan always regretted not having a career. She had worked part time doing fairly mundane things, always hoping that one day a baby would magically appear. She had spent hours looking at baby clothes, equipment and toys in magazines, just in case a miracle happened.

She heard a key in the front door latch. It was Elbaz. He dumped his school ruck sack on the kitchen floor and held out his hand. "For you," he said. Jan stared at him.

"Please," he said thrusting a small clay vase into her hand.

"Oh, Elbaz, thank you. Did you make it?"

He nodded.

Jan clutched the little vase as if it was the most precious thing she had ever held.

About the author
Jo Dearden trained as a journalist with the *Oxford Mail and Times*. She did a degree in English Literature with creative writing as a mature student. She then co-edited her local village newsletter and also worked for the Citizens' Advice Bureau. She is a member of a creative writing group in Suffolk and has written a number of short stories for CafeLit. She is now working on her first novel.

Fishing in Troubled Waters

Linda Flynn

Only a bold plan will remove the outsider from the fishing community, but is it worth the risk?

Dawn rose in a bloodied mackerel-coloured sky over Clovelly Harbour. The cottages huddled together in clusters, flanked either side of a steep cobblestone hill and shouldering only a side view of the sea, as though afraid to stare into its mortiferous depths.

Inside a cottage tucked into the bottom of the hill, Edna tied fish hooks on to thin lines with cracked, red hands. Her coarse brown skirts were runched up around her legs. She glanced at Peter's boots by the door, ready for him to be away with the tide. As the thud of his footfall on the stairs ceased, she looked towards him with dark beseeching eyes. "Will you be taking Rufus with you this time?"

He roughly shook his head, "You know we don't take men on the boats when they've been drinking."

"Yes, I know Peter," her face looked gaunt and shadowy in the silvery light, "but Rufus is often found drinking. Without his catch the family will surely starve."

Peter looked away. "He should know better than to waste it all on porter!"

"But Mary has those bairns to feed and another on its way."

He rammed a foot into a boot, "She chose him. She should never have married that man!"

Edna lowered her voice, "He's new to these parts, not one of our own. Mary mistook a fish eye for a pearl."

Peter raked his hands through his dishevelled black hair. "We never take him when he's like this. He's a danger to the men and the boat."

155

Edna thought of Mary's stooped, shivering body, the dark furrows gathering in puckers across her young face. Her shrieks carried in the wind and mingled with the screams of the gulls and the crashing of the waves. "You heard him shouting in the night, Peter. She needs time to recover. Mary's screams chill my bones, for one day he will knock her stone dead."

"No good will come from this! He'll be an ill omen aboard the boat!" Peter slammed shut the wooden door.

For a moment she stared at it, to settle her breathing, before rising to continue her work.

Edna fastened the crayfish baskets, clambering over rocks and securing them in nooks and crannies. She patted Mary's shoulder as they worked side by side, her baby strapped around her middle. Edna glanced across and saw the beginning of a purplish black mark across her jaw line, before even the previous yellowish blur had time to fade. It could not be hidden by the limp, pale hair that circled around her face.

Neither of them spoke as they watched the fishing boat which bobbed impatiently for the seven men to clamber aboard. Flurries of foam flipped up the side of the wooden hull. An albatross circled and swooped low, giving a shrill cry.

On the quay side, facing the sea, the women spread out in front of trestle tables spread with gleaming piles of herrings. Against the thrashing of the waves was the flashing of sharp blades, slicing the silver fish sideways and slapping them down.

As evening fell, Edna took a lantern up to the cliff top to look out across the Ocean. The clouds bunched up into a brooding, bruised sky. Waves reared up and smashed against the intransigent cliffs, the spray flicking like spittle.

Edna recalled the time that she saw Rufus meandering along the cliff path and how she had hastily swung around and retreated in a different direction, eager to escape his florid face and burnished beard, which was always bristling with anger.

Darkness dropped quickly as she scrambled down the scree, shooting pebbles out from beneath her feet. It was a night without a moon, the sea lost in its own inky depths. She shuddered and drew her cloak around her.

The cottage shutters clattered in the increasing south-westerly wind, which wound its way down the chimney, whistling, whining and ululating. A chill crept around the room as she tossed on her straw mattress. Flickering behind her eyelids Edna thought of Peter. Would six fishermen be enough to restrain Rufus' temper? Had she placed an ill-omened curse upon the vessel? None of the men could swim. She thought of the slippery deck, the vertical drop and dive of the waves which thrashed the boat about.

Her sleep became battered and broken by the sound of the thunderous sea, creaking timbers and a sound like a distant wailing. Even the cottage seemed to shudder and groan as she moaned in her sleep.

Dawn broke strangely calm, as though the sea had spent all of its fury. Edna scrunched along the shingle beach strewn with driftwood, as a pale, watery yellow sun seeped into the sky.

She held her breath as she scanned the horizon. It was bare, with no trace of a boat. Nothing. Just the keening and susurration of the waves.

Shadowy silhouettes of the wives left their cottages on the hill and stood looking out. Like wraiths they fanned out and drifted in formation across the beach, to mend the nets in watchful silence. The women knew well the pattern of

157

the tides, the vagaries of the weather and the hidden dangers concealed in coves or needle ended rocks jutting out along the coast line.

As a veil drew over the long day, Edna made a broth for her supper. She curled herself by the hearth, seeking comfort in the lapping flames.

Some sound must have awoken her, for she sat up rigidly in her chair. A log had capsized onto the flagstone floor where it lay, hissing and sizzling.

Then she heard it again, she was certain. Her heart thumped as she wrapped her shawl around her shoulders and heaved the wooden door open. Edna turned towards the bay and gasped. Buffeted by the waves, moored the fishing vessel, its limp sails curled languidly in the bow.

So where was Peter? She swung around and looked upwards. Only six stooped figures staggered up the hill as though they had lead in their boots.

Edna clung to her door frame as each figure peeled off into one of the houses, until she was standing alone. Solitary as a post. Frozen.

If she hadn't entreated Peter to take Rufus, he might be returning to her hearth. Now she had lost everything. A deep hollowness gnawed her inside.

Then she saw the door of Mary's cottage open and a man stepped out. Like a sleepwalker he drifted back down the hill. "I had to tell her!" he called out. "We lost him around Morte Point. I couldn't let her and the bairns keep waiting, without knowing that we would provide for them."

Edna looked up into his salt-encrusted cracked skin, which had lined into hard ridges. He had returned. For this night at least, he was safe from the sea. Her knees collapsed beneath her and she sat on the cold stone step.

In a distant field she heard the shriek of a fox.

About the author

Linda Flynn has had two humorous novels published: *Hate at First Bite* for 7–9 year olds, and *My Dad's a Drag* for teenagers. Both won Best First Chapter in The Writers' Billboard competition. Her children's book, *A Most Amazing Zoo*, has been released by Chapeltown Books.

She has six educational books with the Heinemann Fiction Project. In addition she has written for a number of newspapers and magazines, including theatre reviews and several articles on dogs.

Linda has had twenty short stories published for adults, children and teenagers. She has also been editing for Bridge House Publishing.

Linda's website is: www.lindaflynn.com.

Number Twenty-seven

Anne Forrest

If I don't get that mortgage, I'm done for! She lit another cigarette. I daren't think about it, I really daren't. But of course she did: I've completed all the forms, Lou's given me a reference, I've cashed in my treasures and my rainy-day fund, but if that chap at Westland says no, then, I'm well and truly done for!

Franny Law sat at her usual table in the Magdala, she even said a little prayer hoping that she'd be granted the means to stay at Number Twenty-seven Wellington Place, and then alongside the prayer, she cursed at her landlord: damn blasted Jewboy wanting to sell. Sell, after all this time!

"What thanks do I get after all these years, eh?"

"What's that, darlin?"

"Nothing, Joey, I was jabbering to myself. Give us another will ya, sweetheart. Make it a double."

"Coming up, Franny." Joey slid her a glass of gin, cleared the ashtray in one swoop and said without looking at her, "What's up with Franny today, eh? Y'look as if you've lost a shillin' and found sixpence."

"Something like that, Joey, something like that…" and she went on as if Joey had access to her thoughts. "I've looked after that bleedin' house all these years – all four floors of it. And how many lodgers, eh! How many? I've lost count. Flotsam and Jetsam most of 'em. Comin' an' goin' like the tide."

"What's that?"

"My lot. At Number Twenty-seven. It's their home for Gawd's sake."

Joey stopped wiping the tables. "What you on about, Franny?"

160

"Goldie's going to sell."

"Is he by gum? Selling is he?"

"He is, the bastard."

"Sign of the times, Franny, sign of the times. Wish I had a house to sell so I do."

Number Twenty-seven had always drawn a mixed bunch; the more memorable ones were not far from Franny's mind these days: she smiled when she thought about Monsieur Pithon, it was him who said they lived in a commune; we weren't just lodgers, he'd said, we were family.

He called me, Mama-matriarch, well of course I was. Who else'd fit the bill? Even though he was a year or two older than me, he used to say it was like them having a mother figure and I would do very nicely thank you, until proper family came to take us to live with them. I went along with all this, 'course I did; they had to have some dignity, didn't they, poor sods? Froggy died in the hospital three years ago. I still miss him. And he was right, we were a little commune, still are, mind you, though a bit depleted these days, only seven of us, ten if you count the cats – that's another thing, if we get re-housed, they might not allow pets – and what if they send us away from Camden? There'll be so many life-changes – it doesn't bear thinking about!

Many of my lodgers just drifted away, y'know, and you never knew if or when they might turn up again; others stayed for the duration, take Emmy Watson and her friend Gina, they've been at Number Twenty-seven for eighteen years. And then there's Trixie; she'll never manage on her own. I admit the house is shabby, needs a lot doing to it; a hell of a lot to be honest, but it's home to us, isn't it? Home. And for them that had no family, it suited fine.

Franny fingered her necklace, ran her little finger round a diamond ring. Held her bejewelled hand away from her, looked at it, head on one side. Nice. They set her hands off nice, especially with a bit of that new nail varnish. Admiring her jewellery, she remembered how glamorous Leah Dobbs thought she looked in her string of pearls with earrings to match. Poor Leah Dobbs, she was a harmless old soul so she was. And ancient Mrs Beddows! She didn't flash her money around buying fancy brooches and hat pins. No, she was careful with her dosh, God love 'er. The gin settled Franny a bit. She grew maudlin. As she reminisced, her eyelids closed.

A draft from the door woke her, along with the chatter of late office-leavers. She saw it was seven thirty-six on the wall clock. Westlands were writing to her today, the letter was in the post room now, being sorted. It would be delivered first thing tomorrow morning, and by eight forty-five she'd know how the land lay. She'd know then if she'd been granted the mortgage, know if she could buy Number Twenty-seven. It's all in the lap of the gods, she said to herself. But what she does now know for certain, is that if she can't purchase the place, someone else will, and Leah Dobbs, Mrs Beddows and three other old souls'd be found dead. Propped up in the back of a cupboard and without a thing to their names.

About the author

Anne Forrest lives in the Conwy Valley, North Wales.

After gaining a First Class Hons at Bangor Uni: MArts in English Literature with Creative Writing, she recently completed a Masters at the University of Chester: Writing and Publishing Fiction 2019-2020.

Her common-folk biography, *My Whole World, Penmaenmawr*, was published by Old Bakehouse Publications, Abertillery, in 2000. Anne's Gothic novel *Lilies of the Valley* made the strong longlist in the Cinnamon Press Debut Novel Award 2019. *Cautiously Tiptoeing...Out of the Light*, a themed collection of short stories written by Anne Forrest and Judy Price, was published on Amazon Kindle and in paperback in September/October 2020.

Timothy Crumble and His Family, a series of six stories set in the National Trust's Bodnant Garden, to educate and entertain children, is being published in the spring 2021.

More of her work can be seen at http://anneforrestwriter.weebly.com and on FaceBook at Forrest & Price.

Rising from the Ashes

Dawn Knox

Drops of rain pitter-pattered on the scorched, mangled metal which had once been Amy's roof. The storm was welcome but it would've been more useful if it had arrived several weeks before, during the height of the drought. Such a deluge might not have halted the bushfire which had swept through the small township of Warringa, but it might have prevented it from escalating to the inferno which had capriciously consumed one building, yet spared another. Such blazes were common around Warringa at this time of year but Amy's neighbour, Peggy, who'd been born in the township eighty-nine years before, had never experienced anything like it.

And now, like Amy, Peggy had lost her home and everything in it to the bushfire. *"Warringa!"* the elderly lady scoffed. "What a joke!"

The town's name was an Aboriginal word, meaning "Cool Place".

Peggy had looked after the newly-weds, Amy and Mike, when they'd arrived from Sydney, thirty years before – young and eager to build their own house and start a family. Twins, Ben and Josh, had been born several years later but at age eighteen, they'd left for Sydney and had not returned. Amy and Mike had stayed in Warringa, missing their sons, but content in the idyllic backwater, in the house they'd built together.

And now, here at Amy's feet, lay the twisted, tangled remains of everything they owned. A buckled saucepan lay next to the charred skeleton of a chair. It alone remained whilst its companions and the table they'd

164

surrounded had been reduced to ashes by the fickle flames. Incongruously, in the garden, the stone birdbath appeared untouched.

Amy stared at the rubble where her piano had once stood. Throughout her life, music had been a constant companion and her mind had always been filled with melodies which had welled up from her soul. But at the sight of the smouldering ruins, the music faltered and died. Now, the only sound she could hear was the staccato beat of raindrops on the corrugated metal which had once been her roof.

She wiped her eyes and turned to go. Other than the birdbath, there was nothing worth salvaging.

Now all she possessed had been donated by others. Members of her community whose properties had been spared by the flames, had been generous to their less-fortunate neighbours and the Red Cross had arrived setting up beds in the school, giving out parcels of necessities and food. Amy had fought back tears when she'd seen how her neighbours had rallied to help, and how outsiders had brought hope.

She was drenched by the time she arrived back at the school where she and Mike had been allocated beds. Ben and Josh had driven their campervan from Sydney that morning to join their father and other volunteer firefighters in tackling the blazes. It was too late for *their* house, of course, but they might save other homes. Amy had been thrilled to see her sons but she'd dreaded them leaving with Mike and the others.

"Don't worry," he'd said, "I'll keep our boys safe."

It would've been selfish to attempt to stop them. All the brave firefighters who'd been combatting the blazes across Australia were someone's son, husband, brother...

165

nevertheless, she'd worry until they were all safe. Thoughts of her men usually made her soul sing, but not now. The sight and stench of the smoking remains of her home filled her mind, leaving no room for music – not even a melancholy tune.

When Amy returned to the school hall, Peggy was sitting on her bed plucking at the crocheted blanket which a well-wisher had donated. Her eyes, which previously had appeared empty as if she couldn't bear to witness more heartache, were now wide open and tear-filled.

"Have you heard from Mike or the boys?" Peggy asked urgently.

Fear gripped Amy's chest, choking her. She shook her head, unable to force words past the lump in her throat.

Peggy put her arm around Amy's shoulders, "I'm sorry, love, but some of the volunteers are missing… I'm sure they'll be all right, though," she added in a trembling voice.

The loss of Amy's home now appeared as nothing, compared to the disappearance of her men. Losing her internal music had been bad enough but now, the silence seemed to slam into her like something solid.

How could she carry on without her family?

Warringa would be restored, the community would rally and help those in need, and life would move forward. But if Mike, Ben and Josh didn't return, Amy could see no future for herself.

That night, she lay on the bed, listening to the snores of those around her. How could she sleep until she had news? When Mike was out fighting bushfires, he always sent her a thumbs-up emoji to tell her all was well if his phone could pick up a signal. But there'd been no messages. That didn't necessarily mean he was in trouble – she knew no news was good news – but across Australia, in the current wave of intense bushfires, several firefighters had died…

She was still awake in the early hours when a truck pulled up outside the school, its headlights slicing through the darkness before dying as the engine stopped. Amy leapt off the bed and barefoot, ran towards the school entrance, hardly daring to hope. At least if it wasn't *her* men, someone might have news of them.

The truck was ghostly in the hazy smoke and darkness but Amy counted five men climb out – stiffly and wearily. Despite the gloom, she recognised Mike, Ben and Josh and with a cry of joy, Amy rushed towards them.

What did it matter if their house had gone? They would build another. The important thing was that she still had her family.

As she hugged her men, she knew she had everything she needed right there in her arms and a joyous melody surged through her mind, filling her soul with music once more.

About the author

Dawn's latest books are *The Macaroon Chronicles* and *The Basilwade Chronicles*, both published by Chapeltown Books. She enjoys writing in different genres and has had romances, speculative fiction, sci-fi, humorous and women's fiction published in magazines, anthologies and books. Dawn has also had two plays about World War One performed internationally.

You can follow her here on https://dawnknox.com.

Circle Time

Rosaleen Lynch

Three girls went missing on three consecutive Fridays after school. Lacey was eleven and her mum didn't report her missing until Justine's disappearance was all over Facebook. Lacey's mum thought she was at her dad's. No one in the neighbourhood believed Lacey's mum, but that's what she told the police. When Milly-Anne went missing, although children still came to Kids Club, they were picked up and dropped off. More than one parent said that it made sense because it was getting dark. Milly-Anne's dad was all over social media within an hour of when he was expecting her home from school. People told him he was overreacting. His answer, twenty-four hours later was a middle finger GIF with the caption "I told you so". He lived on social media from then, even posting pictures of himself answering the door to food deliveries people sent when he tweeted he was too upset to eat. Justine's friends posted new pictures and stories of Justine at regular intervals in the day with messages like "Please come home" and heart and teary-eyed emoticons. Justine's parents prayed.

Circle time at Kids Club started off as normal. We sat in a circle on the carpet and said our names and why we were there. Like I'd say, "I'm Lou-Lou and I'm here to run Kids Club" and the kids would say, "I'm X and I'm here to play" or "I'm Y and I'm here to make friends" and so on. We did that and I asked if anyone had any news to share or if they wanted to talk about anything. It was quiet. We'd talked about everything in this circle from new babies to dead grandmas and it had never been quiet.

"Okay," I said. "I'll start and maybe it's something you

168

might like to talk about. Lacey, Justine and Milly-Anne. I bet some of you are worried?"

There were nods and Mark laughed, "I'm not, it's only girls being taken."

"Mark!"

"Well it's true," he said.

"Mark, I thought you'd be more sensible as you're one of the older ones…"

"But it's true… tell me it's not."

"But what you're saying isn't very kind though is it, when people are worried about their friends. Aren't you worried?"

"Nah, she can take care of herself, anyway she's probably at her dad's."

"Okay, so is anyone worried about the girls?"

Lots of nods.

"Anyone want to talk about it?"

"Maybe they ran off together," Belinda said. "Didn't want to come to my birthday party."

I smiled. "Anyone else?"

Again quiet.

"Okay." I took the bundle of three-inch square pieces of paper I'd got ready. "I'm going to pass round some paper and pens and I want to write down any questions you might have or worries or fears and I'll mix them up and put them in my words so nobody will know who they're from and we can talk about them. And remember your question might be one that others are afraid to ask and you might be helping them out if you ask it."

The group got busy writing, folding and dropping their pieces of paper in the basket in the middle of the circle. A few whispers about how to spell words and a couple of is-it-true-thats and one paper airplane that Mark flew straight into the basket which started others off until everyone wanted to do it even if it meant standing over the basket and dive-bombing.

I opened all the folded planes, and we talked about being afraid of kidnapping. We talked about kids missing their friends. And we talked about not knowing. I went through every comment and question except for one and by the end I was relieved to hear the usual hubbub of six or seven different conversations at once where some had processed and most had moved off the subject onto Belinda's birthday party.

Free-time was a mixture of board games, art, table tennis, pool and video games. We came back to circle time at the end. Lights off and birthday cake in my hands I crossed from the kitchen, singing "Happy Birthday", to where Belinda was sitting on the carpet in the circle. As I swept the room, I saw everyone's eyes focussed on the light of the candles except Mark's. He was looking at me. I bent down and held the cake in front of Belinda as she blew the candles out and the lights came on to applause. Mark stared at me. Belinda cut the cake and handed out pieces.

I went to sit on the floor next to Mark. "What's wrong?"

"Should we be celebrating?" he asked, now not looking at me but at Belinda cutting the cake.

"Yes," I said.

"What are we celebrating though?" he asked looking back at me again.

"Life," I said with a smile.

Mark got up, left the circle, got his coat and stood in the hall ready to go. Belinda didn't let him refuse a piece of her cake and wrapped it in a napkin which he stuffed into his pocket before anyone noticed.

At the end of club all the kids were picked up. Mark's mum was late as usual, even though she'd just crossed the road from the pub. I closed the club door and opened the last piece of paper. I didn't have to check the writing against his class work – I was pretty sure it was Mark's. Not just because there was a little picture of an airplane but because he was a very smart boy, smart enough to play along and smart enough be the pilot he'd grow up to be if he got the chance. That and he had neat hand writing when he wanted it. This time he wanted it. He wrote in clear and urgent capital letters, "take me too".

About the author
Rosaleen Lynch, an Irish community worker and writer in the East End of London, pursues stories whether conversational, literary or performed. Recent publications include the Short Édition story dispensers, The London Reader, Jellyfish Review and Crack the Spine.

Cobalt Blues

Paula R C Readman

A shadow passed over me, as I sat stuffing plastic bags into my father's boots to make them fit. Then someone called my name. I clumsily jumped up, the boots uncomfortable on my feet.

"Good morning, Raoul!" A skinny boy danced just outside the doorway to my shanty home. Dust rose blemishing his shiny black trainers.

"Good morning, Abebe." The crisp whiteness of his shirt held a promise of escape for my friend. I bit back my jealousy and smiled. Over his shoulder, black clouds gathered on the horizon, threatening rain. By the time it arrived, Abebe would be at his desk.

"I'm top of my class now," he stated, pride reflected in his eyes. He lifted the rucksack's straps from his shoulders. The weight of the books caused them to dig in. "I've learnt how to write my name, and my numbers too. That is good, do you not think?"

"Oh yes." Envy buzzed around me. I too wanted to learn.

"Come on, Abebe. You don't want to be late!" The boy's father waved to me. I acknowledged him with a nod. Abebe ran laughing after his father. His laughter was infectious. It made me wish all the children in the village could join him. As they disappeared around a mountain of grey and red soil, I recalled how six years ago our home had faced a lush green valley. Mother, along with the other women, used to sing as they carried their washing down to the river. Birdsongs filled the cobalt-blue sky along with their beautiful voices. Then the miners came.

Overnight, things changed. The once crystal waters

172

became sluggish and murky and no longer providing fish to feed the villagers. The muddy trickle made mother and some of the women sick, too. Across the scarred and poisoned land, the only sounds we heard were the heavy earth-moving machinery as it tore open another mine.

After Mother passed away, Father had to work at the mine. No longer able to hunt, or fish to feed us. The strenuous work and little food weakened him making him more vulnerable to the sickness that engulfed our village. At eleven, I took his place at the mine while my younger brothers kept an eye on him.

"Raoul, be wise. Cover your mouth, hold your tongue, and listen carefully. Never fight," Father said every day before I set off to work. "Come straight home."

"I will, Father." I bent and kissed his forehead. His thinness worried me. I picked up a bag containing bottled water and a small chunk of fufu. My brothers waved me off, and I joined the other men heading to the mine. Ahead of me, the laughter of a few lucky children filled the air as they ran alongside their fathers. At the path's crossroad, they hugged briefly before going their separate ways. I followed the men, while nibbling on a small piece of fufu to stave off the hunger.

Every day I wanted to follow the children to learn about writing, so I could become a fixer, to mend my broken community and to find out why so many of the villagers have fallen sick. I rewrapped the fufu to save for later. If I could earn enough, I would send my brothers to school where they could have a meal every day.

At the mine, bare-footed children younger than me were already working. Women sat cross-legged next to piles of soil. A handful at a time, with lightning speed, they pick out the smallest pieces of cobalt and separate it from the nickel and copper. I went to join them. They nodded their acknowledgements, their eyes still focussed on the dirt in their rough hands. When rain started, lightly at first, they seemed unfazed, and worked on.

After wrapping my cloth bag around my neck, a man lifted a sack full of cobalt onto my shoulders, causing me to bend under its weight. The rain bounced off the ground sending up showers of mud. Once the sack settled in the centre of my back, I gingerly moved forward, trying not to slip. The heavy rain had turned the mine into a sea of mud, rocks and stones.

"Raoul, wait!"

I waited for Imamu. Together, we looked out for each other while avoiding a warren of holes and tunnels as we stumbled our way towards the waiting men with bikes. They loaded up their bikes until it seemed impossible for them to ride. As a man lifted Imamu's sack down, the ground begun to shake violently, causing me to tumble backwards. For a moment, everything went quiet.

I pulled myself up just as a gaping black hole opened. Imamu shouted, but his words were lost as a river of mud and rocks sucked him, the man and his bike in. I screamed and began to dig with my hands, but it was useless as more mud rushed in.

"Get back to work!" the Chinese owner shouted. "Customers are waiting!"

Reluctantly, we returned to our work. As the mine owner oversaw the recovery of Imamu and the man, I asked him. "Please what is Co... balt used for?

"Battery... makes it rechargeable. You understand?" He pointed to his phone.

I nodded.

"Computer, cars... known as clean energy. It's good. Yes."

"Green power." I'd heard the term.

"Yes, no more dirty air to breathe. Everyone healthy. Better for the planet. You learn at school."

"I can't afford schooling."

"A smart boy like you should go to school. You're the only one to ask questions. Not just take the money. It's sad boy and man dead. Now back to your work."

As I waited in line to buy the flour for our evening meal, I thought about my friend, Imamu. Green energy may make a better world, but my people were dying. Now was the time for me to become a fixer so I bought a notebook and pencil. Later, I'll ask Abebe to show me how to write.

About the author

Since 2010 Paula has been published by English Heritage, Bridge House Publishing, Springbok Publications, Parthian Books, Black Hare Press, Blood Song Books, Kandisha Press and Chapeltown Books. In 2012, she was the overall winner of World Book Day short story competition run by Austin Macauley publishers, and Writing Magazine/ Harrogate Crime Writing Festival short story competition, too. In 2020 she had her first crime novella *The Funeral Birds* published by Demain Publishing, followed by *Days Pass Like a Shadow* published by Bridge House, and *Stone Angels* published by Crooked Cat.

Blog: https://paularcreadmanauthor.blog

Book Club for the Elderly

Hannah Retallick

Some people believe that a community consists of likeminded individuals. That's what I thought too, until ours changed my mind: Book Club for the Elderly. That isn't the group's official title, but it might as well be. It's run by a smug young person for the purpose of staving off the inevitable loneliness and misery of the older generation. Pah!

To be fair, though, I am that person: an old, lonely, misery. I've had a run of bad luck this year and it's not even June – who knows what other traumas await me? Firstly, my dear grump, Robert, died after a long battle with a brain tumour. Secondly, my beloved cocker spaniel, Martin, a disgustingly stinky animal, also popped his clogs. His untimely demise somehow managed to extract more tears from me than my husband's. Thirdly, my friends disappeared when my time and emotional energy were taken up with Robert's illness. Tragic, I know.

So, there I was, an old, lonely, misery, with no husband and no dog and nothing to do apart from read.

The book club is advertised for retired people and takes place in a charming corner of Waterstones, a shop in which I spend as much time as possible, because they all know me in there and don't mind when I treat the place like a library. To clarify, I don't take the books home with me – I simply find a comfortable corner, read as much as possible before closing time, make a note of the page number on the back of a receipt, and return to it the following day.

One of the staff, a nice young chap called Gary, was the first to suggest I attend the book club. Once I'd seen three posters and had been cajoled by yet another member of staff, I finally gave in.

We read one book a week, form a staunch opinion, and sit in a circle on a Tuesday evening, forcing our opinion on others. Ruth, whom I unfairly described as a smug young person, is in fact a charming student who took us on as part of a community project that counts in some way towards her university course. Nervy but competent. She'll be with us until the end of the month, at which point we'll take turns choosing books and leading discussions, as we have decided we must continue. It's the only subject on which we all agree. As I implied previously, the community we've formed is anything but likeminded.

There's a cranky git called Malcolm. He must be pushing ninety, is bitter about everything, and blames his aches and pains and misfortunes on everyone apart from himself. He only likes the classics.

A woman called Valerie could be described as the "anti-Malcolm"; she is relentlessly positive, annoyingly so, but the annoyance is because she's impossible to dislike. She's the only person I know with curlier hair than mine. She flirts with Malcolm and teases him, and he pretends not to like it. She loves romance and the genre strangely referred to as "women's fiction".

Catrin and Seren are twins. They're friends of Valerie's and were roped in after the first week. They don't look old enough for retirement. Perhaps they joined the group under false pretences; we should ask for ID. They're always sleek and groomed, with shoulder-length dyed auburn hair and polished nails – a different shade each week. They both love historical fiction and Seren has a worrying fascination with crime and horror.

There's the retired botanist, Steven (loves books about flowers – who would have thought it?), the retired nurse, Martha (mostly interested in outer space, weirdly), and the retired English Literature teacher, Dawn (detects hidden

177

meanings in whatever we read). We feel as if Dawn has an unfair advantage. She doesn't hold inflexible views though and always asks us questions as she might have done with her students.

So, that's us: a group of misfits. My favourite meeting so far was last week's, when everything "kicked off" worse than usual, as Ruth put it to me afterwards, looking a little shaken. Poor child. She does well to hold it together, bless her heart. Anyway, it "kicked off".

The book was a charmingly light story about first love – I can't remember the title, but it was nice enough, an easy read. Malcolm, who is always the first to force his staunch opinion on us, made some comment about how it wasn't "real literature"; Dawn was "inclined to agree"; Valerie huffed (probably for the first time in her life) and said, "You're book snobs." Catrin and Seren picked opposite sides in the debate, crossed their arms, and muttered insults to each other; and the rest of us sat back in our chairs, enjoying the whole thing immensely. They were like clucking hens. Ruth eventually stopped trying to interject, letting the loud and vehement "discussion" run its course.

Odd though it may sound, our bickering community invigorates me and gives me hope. I still describe myself as an "old, lonely, misery"; it was true before, but now I say it ironically, which I imagine comes across in the flippancy of my tone. I have much to thank the book club for, particularly on thrilling evenings where things "kick off". I can't wait for the next meeting. When it comes to anti-aging techniques, I think arguing is hugely underrated.

About the author
Hannah Retallick is a twenty-six-year-old from Anglesey, North Wales. She was home educated and then studied with the Open University, graduating with a First-class honours degree, BA in Humanities with Creative Writing and Music, before passing

her Creative Writing MA with a Distinction. She was shortlisted in the Writing Awards at the Scottish Mental Health Arts Festival 2019, the Cambridge Short Story Prize, the Henshaw Short Story Competition June 2019, and the Bedford International Writing Competition 2019.

https://ihaveanideablog.wordpress.com/

Growing Pains

Theresa Sainsbury

"Matthew. Come here please."

As the boy scraped back his chair, his elbow nudged a water bottle off the corner of his desk. It thudded to the floor. He bent down to pick it up, and at the same time a rubber arched across the classroom and hit him on the back. I shot up out of my seat and crossed my arms. I had a set of classic teacher postures, employed whenever I needed to let the class know I meant business. The sniggers, from mouths chock-full of braces and stale chewing gum, tailed away. I glared at the offenders and their heads snapped back down to their books. They kept chewing. I was pretty sure gum and braces was a lethal combination, but it was up to their parents to sort that problem out. I had enough trouble teasing a decent sentence out of most of them.

Matthew ignored it all and walked towards me. He was loose limbed with a slight bounce in his step and moved with more confidence and purpose than most of the kids who tormented him. There was a glimmer of hope there. Then I remembered how the staffroom weren't much more enlightened about him than his peers.

How come he works so well for you?

Can't get him to listen.

Eyes fixed on the window.

Hardly ever hands in homework.

Will flop in all the exams.

I think he likes English, I said simply.

I sat back down, and Matthew slotted in next to me. He was a couple of inches too close, a tangle of skinny legs and arms. There was a sprinkling of raw-looking spots around his jawline. I could smell the washing powder his mum had used on his school jumper, could hear his slightly laboured breathing. I wondered if asthma needed to be added to his ever-expanding list of issues.

The troublemakers had stopped talking. We were in Room 120, with the big picture windows and the classroom was greenhouse hot. The kids were getting drowsy.

"You've written about a different poem to everyone else Matthew," I said.

"Yes."

"Any reason for that?"

"I liked it."

"Okay. But if you did that in the exam, it might be a problem."

"But it wasn't the exam, it was homework."

He is pedantic, which could indicate he suffers from mild Asperger's Syndrome. I could see his Special Needs report floating in front of me. I disagreed with most of it. He was shy, awkward with strong ideas. Can't anyone be a bit different these days?

I tried another tactic. "Didn't you like the poem I set?"

"It was alright. But the one I wrote about is better."

"Why?"

"Because it's more important."

"What do you mean?"

He stared straight ahead; his eyes looked glassy.

"Your poem talked about the war in a physical way, about wounds and dead bodies. They were the obvious things. People either healed or died. Mine was about how it affected their minds. That was invisible and my great grandad never recovered."

A silence settled in as I thought about what to say next. He concentrated on his lump of blu-tack, a gift from the Special Needs Department to help him concentrate. He

181

circled it between his palms, using slow, hypnotic movements.

"Would you read it – your essay – to the rest of the class? Next week maybe."

He sucked in the hot air between his teeth, pushed his index finger into the plasticine-like ball and prodded it.

"I'll record it miss. I'm rubbish at reading. And I don't want them to laugh."

"Yes, that's a good idea."

"I might get Mum to do it. She's got a nice voice."

"Great."

"And I'll bring my prop in too, the stuff my great grandad brought home." And with that he swiped his book and returned to his desk. I had been politely dismissed.

The class were too sozzled by the sun to notice him this time.

The audio file was attached to the email that pinged into my inbox. I clicked on it. The voice was newsreader quality, crisp and professional. His mum. She'd keep my class of semi-delinquents awake.

At the end of the first paragraph she paused.

A gunshot powered through my headphones.

I jumped.

A high-pitched scream, a low groan.

He'd set a trip wire for them and added sound effects. Another pause and the female voice continued, more urgent now. The hairs on the back of my neck were up.

I tried to picture the class. Their reaction. I tried to picture him too, but his face wouldn't come together.

Noise reverberated around Room 120 on the afternoon when Matthew's story got told. As guns fired and screams and sirens soared, the teenagers, who were arranged on chairs in a messy circle around my desk, grabbed each other's arms, clamped hands over their ears and screamed back.

At the end, it would have been enough to lead them in a congratulatory clap to firmly alter Matthew's status forever. But I wanted more. I persuaded him to talk about his prop himself.

He stood up next to my desk and produced a small, crackly paper bag.

"Inside this bag is some earth. The same earth that you get everywhere, only this came from the battlefield, from the ground next to where my great grandad's pilot lay dead."

The kids craned their necks. A couple stood up to get a better view.

"Surviving is sometimes more difficult than dying," he said solemnly as he shook some of the sand into a glass dish.

I caught sight of one of his bullies. He gave me the slightest of nods and unclenched his jaw. In that moment he seemed to relax his hold on the rest of the pack. He was the first to step forward to peer into the dish.

The class changed that day. They never went back to how they were.

About the author
Theresa Sainsbury writes to make sense of things; from complications in her past to concerns about the future. Last year she finally plucked up courage to apply to do a Creative Writing MA. She was terrified she might not get accepted (she only has English O' level) and equally terrified when she was! She now has a fledging novel tucked away, but short stories are her first love. She was published by both Mslexia and Bradt Travel in 2019.

Books and the Barbarians

Allison Symes

"What good will Sparos be coming with us, Derentia? He throws up on every dimension jump trip," Resmos told his co-pilot.

Resmos glared at the forlorn seven stones weakling who stood at the time machine's steps.

"Sparos finds things useful to our tribe." Derentia beckoned to Sparos to come up. "Discovering how to make fire was useful. We now all enjoy hot food."

Resmos swore. "Okay but you clear up if he's sick this time. What the hell is wrong, Sparos? Don't you know what hoops we've had to go through to get the permissions needed for you to come with us? You repay us by vomiting!"

"I don't know, Resmos, sir. I've not been right since I was a kid. You know that."

Resmos laughed mirthlessly. "Well, you're honest."

"I couldn't help being ill, Resmos, sir. Everyone had that sickness."

"Only you never went on to grow strong. Picking up sticks would be too much for you."

Sparos bowed. It was his rotten luck to be born into a species prizing physical strength.

The virulent illness that swept through his tribe, killing many, left him with a physique that was not only undesirable (as the females all made clear), but made him the butt of every weakling joke imaginable.

So, he had to justify his continued existence. By finding things the community found useful, he'd gained the nickname The Scavenger, but there was grudging respect behind it.

Sparos swore Resmos wouldn't know what might be useful if it hit him. What was it about being muscular that led to not being able to think? Mind, there was nobody else you'd want on your side in a fight with an alien species.

"You weren't sick, well done," Resmos said as the trio headed home. "Why couldn't you have managed that before?"

Sparos smiled. Even that was weak. "I didn't eat anything this time, Resmos, sir."

"That explains your grumbling stomach," Resmos replied. "I swear that could've been heard in Alpha Centuri! What have you found this time?"

Derentia gave Sparos an encouraging smile.

Sparos sighed. "Stories, Resmos, sir."

"We have stories. You are the tribal storyteller. What do you want more for?"

"These are written tales. The others I have to remember." Sparos held up a red leather book and flicked open the pages. "This has pictures in it."

Resmos grunted. "It looks nice. I like a good story. But that doesn't look as if it is in our language for the good reason we don't have a written one. You do remember you're an oral storyteller?"

Sparos blushed. "Yes, Resmos, sir, but the universal translator I found on that abandoned planet we visited last time should decipher this. We can have a wider range of stories to enjoy. Our winters are long enough."

Derentia grunted. "Yes, the Earth equivalent of thirty years. Not fun. I hope the stories you've picked are good. We need the entertainment. Nobody felt like laughing after that sickness."

"Give Sparos his due, Resmos," Derentia said, "he is on to something with this book idea. The stories are great though I still don't believe a tortoise could win a race, not with legs like that. Everyone loved the pictures."

185

"We only have Sparos's say-so those words he says the universal translator translated are what's on those pages."

"Even if he made it up, why would the translator do so? He's not clever enough to fix that."

"True but it shouldn't just be Sparos who can read those books."

"I must learn to read first, Resmos," Sparos said. "I'm reliant on the universal translator too."

"Get on with it, lad. Then teach us. Do you think I just want to be known for my muscles? It would be nice to do something clever. It would impress the females for a start."

Sparos brightened.

"Not for a weakling, my lad."

Sparos frowned. "I'll need someone to teach me to read, so I can teach everyone else."

"No. Just me, lad."

Derentia coughed. "No, everyone learns to read. If you think, Resmos, you're getting away with trying to impress the females like that, then know I'll learn to read and impress the males." Derentia laughed. "I thought you wouldn't like that. You should see your face! If we all read, we all know if Sparos has been reading the stories correctly."

"But…"

"But me no buts," Derentia said. "Hmm… catchy that. I've heard it somewhere. Sparos, you come with us tomorrow. We'll return to Earth and find a teacher. Then we teach everyone else. It'll give us something useful to do this winter instead of fighting amongst ourselves because we're cooped up."

"I never expected that," Resmos said.

Derentia shrugged. "Getting through the winter without

fighting is a first. Secondly, we now know Sparos is a good storyteller and was reading those books correctly."

"Did he expect everyone to write their own stories and read them out?"

"How could he? Nobody anticipated that but writing also kept the tribe quiet. See Sparos over there. He's set himself up as a consulting editor, whatever that is. He said he discovered the phrase on Earth but everyone's hanging on his every word."

"He's dating several females. Is he giving them good verdicts on their stories in return for…"

Derentia grinned. "Good luck to him if he is. Resmos, you'd have done something like that at his age. There's more to our seven stone weakling son than meets the eye!"

Resmos grinned. "What did Sparos want bringing back?"

"As many writing materials as we can stuff in the cargo hold. Let's steal stationery! Now there's something I never expected to say!"

"Sparos said some places ban reading. I can see why."

"Our species may be muscular and considered thick, but we have open minds. Let's go. I've got short stories to edit when we return."

Resmos groaned. "I'm cooking again then?"

"Yes. That book Sparos read about role reversal was so interesting!"

About the author

Allison Symes is published by Chapeltown Books, CaféLit, and Bridge House Publishing amongst others. She is a member of the Society of Authors and Association of Christian Writers. She adores reading and writing quirky fiction. Her website is https://allisonsymescollectedworks.com and she blogs weekly for online magazine, Chandler's Ford Today, often on writing related topics:
http://chandlersfordtoday.co.uk/author/allison-symes/.

Index of Authors

Mehreen Ahmed, 134
Gail Aldwin, 32, 102, 138
Michael Baez, 127
RBN Bookmark, 60
Christopher Bowles, 56, 111, 140
Amelia Brown, 84
J S Brown, 50, 73
Beverley Byrne, 88
Maxine Churchman, 145
Jeanne Davies, 77, 148
Jo Dearden, 152
Linda Flynn, 47, 70, 155
Anne Forrest, 160
Jenny Gibson, 29
Katie Granger, 11
Jessica Joy, 96
Dawn Knox, 38, 164
Sinéad Kennedy Krebs, 98
Irene Lofthouse, 67
Rosaleen Lynch, 168
Madeleine McDonald, 123
Linda Morse, 15
James Morton, 52
Julia Norman, 34
Daniel Paton, 62
Helen Price, 80
Alison Rayner, 21
Paula R C Readman, 25, 92, 172
Hannah Retallick, 120, 176
Louise Rimmer, 116
Theresa Sainsbury, 180
Allison Symes, 44, 108, 184
Marion Turner, 42
Yvonne Walus, 104

Other Publications by Bridge House

Nativity

edited by Debz Hobbs-Wyatt and Gill James

Many of the stories in this collection take place at or near
Christmas time. There are stories of new births, of rebirths,
of new beginnings, and there are a couple that deal with the
joys and sorrows of the annual Nativity Play.

There are some familiar authors in this volume and also some
new writers. We treasure them all.

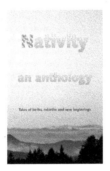

"A most unexpected collection of stories, focused on new
beginnings and rebirth. It's definitely not your traditional
nativity theme, but so much more. The stories are so varied,
dramatic, melancholic, dark and comedic, there is a story to
suit everyone." (*Amazon*)

Order from Amazon:

Paperback: ISBN 978-1-907335-76-1
eBook: ISBN 978-1-907335-77-8

Crackers

edited by Debz Hobbs-Wyatt and Gill James

Every year we pick a very vaguely Christmas-related theme
for our annual anthology. Then we invite our writers to
subvert it. In this collection, they've certainly done that to
the extent that we almost had a picture of cream crackers for
the cover. Our theme this year is "crackers". So, we have
Christmas crackers, cream crackers, cracking dresses, a
cracked antique and many, many other interpretations. We
hope you will find this a cracking good read.

"A wonderfully quirky and eccentric collection of short stories.
Each one has a different take on the notion of 'crackers' with a
heart of darkness resonating throughout. A book of little
morality gems!" (*Amazon*)

Order from www.bridgehousepublishing.co.uk

Paperback: ISBN 978-1-907335-59-4
eBook: ISBN 978-1-907335-60-0